SHADOWS ON THE WATER

WITHDRAWN

SHADOWS ON THE WATER

Elizabeth Cadell

Chivers Press • Thorndike Press
Bath, Avon, England   Thorndike, Maine USA

This Large Print edition is published by Chivers Press, England, and by Thorndike Press, USA.

Published in 1995 in the U.K. by arrangement with Sir John Cadell & Mrs Janet Reynolds.

Published in 1995 in the U.S. by arrangement with Brandt & Brandt Literary Agents, Inc.

U.K. Hardcover ISBN 0–7451–2657–X (Chivers Large Print)
U.K. Softcover   ISBN 0–7451–2668–5 (Camden Large Print)
U.S. Softcover   ISBN 0–7862–0289–0 (General Series Edition)

The text of this Large Print edition is unabridged.
Other aspects of the book may vary from the original edition.

Set in 16 pt. New Times Roman.

Printed in Great Britain on acid-free paper.

British Library Cataloguing in Publication Data available

Library of Congress Cataloging-in-Publication Data

Cadell, Elizabeth.
   Shadows on the water / Elizabeth Cadell.
     p. cm.
   ISBN 0–7862–0289–0 (alk. paper : lg. print)
   1. Large type books. I. Title.
[PR6005.A225S53 1995]
823′.914—dc20
                                         94–26164

CHAPTER ONE

My brother Henry saw me off—with reproaches.

Why, he asked, couldn't I have waited? Why dash off like that in the middle of December? Why not wait and enjoy a quiet Christmas at home?

'He's my first grandchild; I want to take a look at him,' I said, and forebore to point out that last Christmas—the first since my two children had married and gone abroad—had been very quiet indeed, and I hadn't enjoyed it at all.

'If you'd waited until March,' said Henry, 'they would have come home on leave; you could have seen them—him—without wasting all this money.'

'It won't be wasted,' I promised him. 'Travel's broadening.'

I saw his eyes on my waistline—but it was an absent glance; he wasn't the sort of brother who made sardonic remarks.

The taxi stopped at the station and he handed me out. As my suitcases were put down, I stood between them and Henry, carefully screening the labels from his view. I presented my cheek for his farewell kiss.

'Don't bother to come to the train,' I said. 'It was kind of you to bring me to the station.

Now, you just pop off to the office and—'

'I came,' said Henry, 'to see you into the train.'

That's what he came for, and that's what he meant to do. That was Henry: ponder, plan and perform. I've never understood how two people as completely different as Henry and I could have been born of the same pair of parents. I don't ponder, I rarely plan and if I do perform, it's in a haphazard sort of way. We've only got, I think, one thing in common, and that's a sense of duty, but our ideas of what constitutes duty are widely, wildly opposed.

'Have you your train ticket?' he asked. He had paid the taxi driver and we were walking to the boat train. 'Your passport? The keys to your trunk? Your—'

His words and his steps came to an abrupt stop, and I knew that his glance had fallen on the labels on my luggage. I stood beside him waiting for his reactions, which are slow. When he once grasps a fact, he keeps it forever, but he doesn't grasp very quickly and so I knew that it would take some moments for him to realize the enormity of my offence. While he was looking at the evidence, I looked at him: tall, stout, clean-shaven, middle-aged; neat striped trousers, black coat. He looked what he was: a prosperous City merchant; the bowler hat and rolled umbrella proclaimed the city to be London. He had the fresh, clear skin that is at his age, I suppose, one of the rewards of a

2

well-spent life. He had plenty of sound sense and not one grain of humor.

He turned from his contemplation of my luggage and fixed shocked eyes on me, but he would not speak until he had waved the porter on and we were following, weaving our way through the hurrying, jostling crowd. I could see other porters wheeling barrows on which were piles of luggage with labels similar to those on my own: S.S. *Juan Cortez*; Royal Atlantic Line. Most of the passengers seemed bound, like myself, for Buenos Aires.

'I thought,' said Henry at last, in a suffocated voice, 'that you were going tourist class.'

'No tourist berth,' I said. 'I asked them; they said there wasn't a single tourist berth to be had. I mean, there wasn't one single return tourist—'

'You were, as usual, taken in. It was an attempt—a successful one—to make you buy a first-class ticket.'

'Well, there wasn't another boat with a tourist berth until goodness knows when. I want to see the baby while he's still a baby, after all; I don't want to wait until he's in his teens, do I? I want to see him while he's still in that lovely, cuddly, helpless—'

'How much,' inquired Henry, 'did you pay?'

I told him. It halted him in his tracks, as I knew it would. Stealing a sidelong glance, like the old-time heroines, I saw that he was pale with anguish.

'It isn't,' I said apologetically, 'a de luxe cabin, or anything. It does happen to have a bathroom, but there's someone else in it—in the cabin, I mean. I—'

'You are paying,' intoned Henry, 'this fantasic sum merely to cross the Atlantic to see an infant who is to be brought home by his parents in just over three months' time. You are leaving the prospect of an inexpensive winter here in London in order to—'

'It isn't only the baby,' I lied. 'Think what I'll see: Lisbon, and ... and Buenos Aires, and Sue, and—'

I paused, lost in wonder. Sue ... with a baby. It didn't seem possible. Me, a grandmother. Equally impossible, until I looked at Henry and saw on him the years that I could never feel on myself. Sue ... a mother.

'I cannot imagine,' said Henry, 'what you were thinking of.'

'Well, I hadn't been away for so long,' I said weakly.

'You were in Wales in June. You were in Scotland in August.'

'I meant away—abroad. I was restless, wondering about Sue and—'

'You were restless,' said Henry, walking on in slow march time, 'because all your life you have acted on impulse. You have never paused to think; you have never considered, never weighed. Good heavens, Kate, you speak in one breath of being a grandmother and in the next of squandering large sums of money in order to transport yourself in luxury, in needless luxury—'

'I *asked* for a tourist berth.'

'You will never,' summed up Henry, 'learn the rudiments of sense. Or the rudiments of finance. As long as you live, you will be incapable of saving money. As long as you live—'

'People can hear you,' I said.

That pulled him up at once. Lecturing your sister is one thing; allowing total strangers a glimpse of your private life is another. Henry quickened his pace and walked on with long, angry strides, and I trotted meekly beside him.

'What is the number of your compartment?' he asked.

'Three D.'

'First class, naturally?'

'Yes.'

I sounded sheepish. I felt sheepish. I reminded myself that the money was mine; that I had earned it; that I had a right to spend it as I wished. There was no need for me to cringe, I told myself; I had by my own unaided efforts spun out my husband's meagre income during his lifetime; after his death, I had brought up our two children, paid for their food and clothing and education and thrown in a lot of fun as make-weight. I had done this without availing myself of Henry's offer of assistance. I had, by God and good luck, stood on my own feet and stood the two children up on theirs. One—Nigel—was standing in Canada, and the other—Sue—in Buenos Aires, and I meant to make more than this one trip to see them. The money was mine and not Henry's, and he had not the faintest right to tell me how I should spend it. So there.

I felt more sheepish than ever.

'I needn't remind you,' said Henry, 'that your expenses won't end with the luxury fare. You will sign for drinks—for other people. You will spend money going ashore. You will—'

'I'd like an empty compartment, please.'

'—buy every bit of tourist trash you lay your eyes on. You will—'

'Not that one.' I checked him as he was about to open the door. 'There's somebody in there.' Then, to take Henry's mind off the present, I added: 'An elderly man.'

The words had the desired effect. For Henry, for all his poor opinion of my looks and character, had never lost hope of finding me another husband. Like all men, he had the unshakeable conviction that all woman really needs is a man: a man to support her, to steady her, to restrain her. For fifteen years—ever since my husband died—he had done his best, in ways he considered discreet, to induce me to remarry. So now he forgot his strictures on

6

economy and edged nearer to get a look at the man seated in a corner seat of the compartment.

I could see him relaxing. The man was long and lean and thin and gray-haired and looked serious and intellectual—and prosperous. I could see Henry deciding that perhaps it wasn't, after all, a bad thing that I wasn't going to be stuck away in the tourist class, missing all the moneyed males.

He opened the door; my suitcases were placed on the rack, my rug on a corner seat. Gray-hair, without looking up, edged his hat and papers two inches nearer to his seat and hid himself behind the *Times*.

I stood on the platform with Henry, listening to him as he murmured meaningless phrases about tickets and luggage; then his eyes roved over me, and I saw him frown. In a voice pitched low to avoid being overheard, he addressed me reproachfully.

'If you'd spend more money on your clothes, Kate, and less on other things . . . Your coat—'

'What's the matter with my coat?'

'My dear girl, there's no need to get annoyed. I—'

'I'm not annoyed; I just asked what you didn't like about it.'

'I said nothing, nothing whatsoever about not liking it. I merely thought that it was scarcely a suitable color for a woman of your age and build, and—'

'It's amber, and you yourself told me that amber was a good color for me because my hair was red.'

'I told you that when your hair was still red.'

'All right; it's now a sort of dusty mouse. Anything else?'

'I only felt that the fur looked a little cheap and—'

'Well, perhaps it does. If it does, it isn't surprising, because it was cheap. It was very cheap. I bought it in Petticoat Lane and I hacked it up and stuck it on the coat and I thought it looked very nice indeed, and it's just like you to take all the stuffing out of somebody just when they think they're looking decent and setting off to impress their daughter and—'

'Hush!'

'Hush yourself. Have you anything to say about my hat?'

'Nothing whatsoever.'

'That means you don't like it.'

'I said nothing—'

'Well, I don't like it, either. Your wife gave it to me. And you can tell her that I look a freak in it, as I knew I should. You can—'

'Will you kindly moderate your voice?'

'I am speaking as quietly as you are. Thank you for coming to see me off and for taking away all the fun of the trip before it ever began. I'd like to remind you that I paid for my ticket myself, and I didn't and don't dress to impress

8

you, and I never had any dress sense and never will and—'

I stopped. Henry's face had frozen into agonized embarrassment. Following his glance, I saw that the elderly man was no longer in the compartment; he was standing on the platform, hat on head, newspaper under arm, and his place had been taken by a younger man who now leaned out to say the last good-bys. Henry and I, absorbed in our argument, had failed to observe the changeover, but it was clear that the older man was not traveling; he had either been keeping a seat for the younger one, or he had got into the train to rest while the young man went to buy books and newspapers.

Tight-lipped, Henry handed me into the compartment. There was a shrill whistle and a banging of doors; I leaned down and offered a cheek, and Henry brushed his lips against it. When this passionate exchange was over, he shut the door, stood back and raised his hat as the train began to move.

The next moment something hit him from behind and I saw him stagger. Dignity flown to the wind, he clutched wildly at the air and struggled to regain his balance. Scarcely had he done so when a second blow struck him. But for this one he was more prepared, and I saw him leap with more agility than I would have thought possible out of the path of the porter who was following the boy and girl who had

9

wrenched open the door, and, heedless of the angry shouts of the guard, had leapt into the compartment and were catching the suitcases the porter threw in after them.

There were ten seconds of utter chaos. I crouched in my corner. The young man in the corner, who a few moments before had been seated with almost as much sober dignity as the elderly man had shown, was now on his feet and, with swift presence of mind, had pulled the girl out of the way and was making room for the last of the luggage as the boy flung it in. Then he had taken the money that the girl, too breathless to speak, held out to him; he had put the boy aside and he had leaned out and handed it to the now madly running porter. Then he had seized and closed the door.

They were in.

There were several moments of silence, broken only by the panting of the boy and the girl as they fought to regain their breath.

'Did it!' gasped the boy at last. 'Close thing, Lindy.'

The two made their apologies—very charmingly, I thought. The young man received them with a bow, brushed his coat, sat down in his corner, shook open the *Times* and vanished behind it. The gestures, the attitude were so like those of the elderly man who had occupied the seat, that I guessed them to be father and son—and then I had turned to study the newcomers.

I liked what I saw. The girl was tall and slender and extremely pretty; her voice was light and clear, and she spoke very fast. She was about nineteen—Sue's age—and as attractive ... well, almost as attractive as Sue. But Sue is dark and this girl was fair—ash blond.

The boy was obviously her brother; the likeness between them was strong. He was about sixteen, slim and trim and, in a pleasing way, entirely at his ease. His speech was as deliberate as his sister's was rushed; as they settled themselves, they chatted, and I learned that the boy's name was Rex.

They were a nice pair. I felt a strong but ridiculous impulse to lean over and tap the young man on the knee and tell him what he was missing. He couldn't, I thought, have been more than twenty-six; he was large and well built and had proved a moment ago that he was strong and quick-witted; it was a pity his father had let him grow into a sobersides without an eye for a lovely girl. Far from exhibiting any rise in temperature, he was turning the pages of the newspaper and applying himself to the leading article. Ignoring us completely, he got through the *Times* and started on the *Spectator*. Then he went on to *Country Life*. When he'd got through them all, he folded them neatly, placed them in a pile beside him, leaned back, and looked with intentness at the scenery.

The girl's eyes met mine. Hormone deficiency, I conveyed without words. See if we care, she seemed to say.

She and the boy and I began to exchange civilities. Then the girl brought herself up short in one of her swift rushes of speech.

'Oh—you're Mrs Verney!' she said, and gave me an enchanting smile. 'We're in the same cabin.'

I was grateful for the smile; she knew she was sharing a cabin with me, and she was pleased. My liking for her increased—and then I looked at her in surprise.

'How do you know?' I asked.

'I saw your name on your luggage a moment ago.'

'Yes, but how—'

'I was furious—' she grinned—'at not getting a cabin to myself, and the man at the shipping office promised to get me somebody nice. I was so afraid,' she swept on, 'that I'd get one of those awful people who wake up if you put a light on, and hate one's being in the cabin while they dress, and want the first bath and ... and that kind of thing.'

'What makes you think I'll sleep through everything?'

'Instinct.' She laughed, and the boy laughed with her, and I laughed. We all laughed but young Life-is-earnest in the corner.

'My name's Barron,' went on Lindy. 'Lindy Barron.'

12

I bowed—but for a second my mind was not on her, but on the young man in the corner. He had shot her a swift look as she spoke her name, and I thought he was going to say something. But she had gone on to introduce her brother, and he turned once more to his contemplation of the scenery.

'This is my brother, Rex. We're traveling to Lisbon. You're going on, aren't you, to Buenos Aires?'

'Yes. My daughter's just had her first baby and I can't wait to get out there and make certain that they're bringing him up properly.'

'What's his name?'

'They want to call him Theobald, but perhaps I'll be there in time to save him.'

'Theobald—poor little sweet,' she said warmly.

I saw a slight movement from the corner—a twitch of embarrassment, or it might have been dismay. But Lindy rushed on.

'We're going out to my father; he's got a business in Lisbon. He—'

She stopped. There had been an interruption. A cough. A short, discreet cough from the man in the corner; not bronchial, not asthmatic; simply one of those coughs which indicate that somebody is about to say something.

All eyes on him, we waited.

'I heard you say just now—' His voice was low, pleasant, but, like his appearance, rather serious. 'I heard you say just now that your name was Barron and that—'

'—we were going out to stay with my father. I knew it!' said Lindy triumphantly.

'Knew what?' inquired her brother.

'He's in—' She stopped and turned to the man. 'You're in my father's firm, aren't you?'

'I am.'

'And your name's Harper. Neil Harper.'

'Neil Theobald Harper.'

The quick color came into her cheeks, and she smiled—and then she gave him a long look during which, it was clear, she was measuring what she had heard about him against what she now saw: the portrait against the original.

'Lindy, don't stare,' came from Rex, and the color rose again to her cheeks.

'I'm sorry,' she told Mr Harper. 'It was just—My father said—'

She stopped abruptly, and it became crystal-clear to everybody present that what her father said had not been sufficiently complimentary to repeat. She covered her confusion by standing up and getting a case off the luggage rack. And as Rex rose to help her, and the two had their backs to us, Mr Harper glanced at me, a brief, almost an expressionless glance, but one which raised my spirits.

He wasn't, after all, dead. He was alive; very much so. He was enjoying Lindy, in his way, as much as I was.

But a moment later I was asking myself

14

whether I had imagined it, for he had turned to look out once more at the scenery, and he showed no disposition to join our conversation. There was nothing unfriendly about his attitude; it was simply one of withdrawal, the attitude of the average English traveler who, while having nothing against his traveling companions, prefers to keep himself aloof, apart, unentangled.

We reached Southampton. Mr Harper, having helped Rex with the luggage and seen it assembled neatly on the platform, bowed and took his departure. Lindy watched him go and turned to me with a grin.

'I nearly gave myself away, didn't I?' she said.

'You seemed about to say something indiscreet.'

'She specializes in that sort of thing,' Rex told me. 'When she opens her mouth, and when you know her better, you'll hang on to your seat. She was just going to tell him that my father'd written to say that there'd be a man from his firm on board, and that his name was Harper and that he was strong on brains and death on women.'

'Death?' I repeated in mystification.

'He doesn't know they're there. That kills them,' explained Rex.

'If I'd said it, he wouldn't have cared,' said Lindy. 'Did you ever see anything so completely self-sufficient in all your life?'

I was about to tell her about Henry, but we were going up the gangway, and I remembered suddenly that one day, soon, I'd be walking down it again at Buenos Aires, to find Sue and her husband and the baby waiting.

The cabin was all I had hoped it would be. The bathroom, though tiny, looked full of gleam and shine. The steward and the stewardess came in to introduce themselves; the luggage was brought in.

I unpacked and put away my things. Lindy had vanished, intent on seeing everything, exploring everywhere. I thought about her, and about her brother, and decided that I thoroughly liked them both.

To my surprise, they spent most of their time in my company. Perhaps they felt that a three-day journey was not long enough in which to make it worth while getting to know people. Perhaps, like myself, they found a preliminary survey of the passengers unrewarding. Whatever the reason, they spent the first day and a half with me, walking, talking and intermittently eating—we had seats together at a table for four. The fourth place, we were pleased to find, was vacant; we were a companionable trio, and we felt that a fourth might have proved a disappointment. Lindy and Rex chattered and I listened, as I had listened to Sue and Nigel. One thing about listening is that you can form your own opinions about the people who are talking to you. I formed conclusions about the two young Barrons; I would never, I knew, have the opportunity to test the correctness of my guesses, but it was interesting to make them.

It was their first trip to Lisbon, although their father had been in business there for many years. Without its being actually stated, I gathered that their parents had not lived together; while the mother was alive, these two had lived with her in England. She had been dead for just over a year, and they were making their first visit to their father. Rex was to return to England, to school, after the Christmas holidays; Lindy was staying in Lisbon indefinitely.

We got along very pleasantly until we reached the Bay of Biscay—and then the ship, which had been as steady as a rock, began to roll and then to pitch, and finally developed a circular motion that removed the passengers, as if by magic, from the lounges and the decks and the dining saloon.

I was almost the first down, but I was not seasick. I am an excellent sailor, but when the ship begins to dance, I have to lie down. Once horizontal, I enjoy the movement and can take an intelligent interest in what goes on around me; only when I get to my feet do I remember that I'm at sea.

Rex was an early casualty. Lindy, who seemed to have been born with sea legs, and who showed not the faintest sign of unease, went down to see her brother and came up again to report that he had announced that he was dying, and wished to die alone.

Lindy stayed on her feet, but she was about the only woman who did. The Bay of Biscay is notoriously temperamental, and this was one of its uglier moods. She came back from dinner on the second night at sea to report that the saloon had been almost empty. But the rough weather, which had removed Rex and myself from the table, had produced...

'Who d'you think?' she asked.

'The captain,' I said. 'He always sits at the table of the best people.'

'You mean they always sit at his. No, not the captain—who's terribly dull, anyway,' said Lindy. 'It was Mr Harper!'

'Well, you think he's dull, too, don't you?'

'Dull?' Lindy's voice was high. 'Dull? Aunt Kate, he's ... he's moribund.'

'Didn't he talk at all?'

'He doesn't talk. He opens his mouth, lets out two or three words like a little boy letting pennies out of his money box, and then he shuts it again, bang!'

'Perhaps he feels seasick?'

'Not he! Nobody ever would, he said, if they did as he does: he spends the first day in his cabin, getting acclimatized. He's as well as ... as I am.'

'Perhaps he preferred eating to talking.'

'He ordered steamed sole, and I chose cream

18

of mushroom soup, and lobster—and then he called the steward back and said he'd have lobster, too.'

'That was nice and friendly.'

'Friendly!' Lindy flung herself down on her bed, regardless of her pretty, billowing frock, and waved her feet in the air. 'Friendly? Shall I tell you how the conversation went?'

'Please do.'

'Well, when we'd given our orders, he sat there just looking aloof, like he did in the train.'

'As he did in the train,' I corrected automatically, before I remembered that she wasn't Sue.

'As he did in the train. He crumbled the toast on his plate—melba—and he looked just as dry as the toast did.' She twisted around, raised herself to rest on her elbows, and stared across at me. 'You know what I think? He's been reared on ice and rusks. He's never had any nice, warm, gushing, mother's milk. I bet he's been an orphan from birth.'

'I don't think so. A man saw him off—his father, I'm certain.'

'Well, this man'll never be a father, unless he marries an iceberg and begets a lot of little ice cubes. I said to him—and I threw all my charm into it—"I hope you haven't been ill?" "No, thank you," says he, all short-like.'

'He's your father's employee. Perhaps he feels—'

'Pooh! You can always tell *that* sort of

19

standoffishness. No, it isn't that. I asked him why he hadn't come to meals, and he told me about staying in his cabin for the first day. I said I was glad he'd got his sea legs, and he bowed and said he saw I'd got mine.' She paused to consider. 'Do you suppose he meant anything?'

'No. He doesn't look that kind of man.'

'That's what I thought. So I gave up. I ate, and he ate, and the only sound was the clash of plates and the noise his toast made when he chewed it.' She sighed. 'All that six feet plus of manhood, and not one tiny spark to go with it. All those wasted good looks—there isn't a man on board who's as handsome as he is—and it's just my luck that he has to be stone dead.'

But the next day, when the ship had settled down and I faced Mr Harper across the table, I found myself disagreeing with this estimate of him. He might be aloof, he might sound laconic, but there was something in his eyes that I look for, almost unconsciously, in everybody I meet. If I find it, I feel on firm ground; if it isn't there, I withdraw and seek it elsewhere. I don't know whether it's humor, or kindliness, or just plain humanity; I only know that this man had it. After that, I stopped thinking of him as dull. He was his own man; if he cared to come out of his shell, I thought that he would prove to be an interesting and amusing one.

He sat beside me on deck after lunch; we

20

watched Lindy and Rex playing shuffleboard, and I asked him about their father. Getting any information out of him was difficult; he made, for him, long and informative speeches about the other members of the firm, but about Mr Barron he remained uncommunicative. I respected his discretion, but I felt that under the circumstances it was carried beyond the bounds of necessity.

'What's he like?' I asked for the third time.

'He's a very large man, and some people consider him handsome. One of the senior partners in the firm might interest you, if you have time to meet him when the ship stops in Lisbon. Fellow named Cunha. Portuguese, and very—'

'I gather,' I said, 'that Mr Barron and his wife didn't live together.'

'No; not for the greater part of their marriage. No divorce; separation.'

'They're nice children. He must have missed them.'

Without saying a word, without even a sign; merely by lighting his pipe, Mr Harper succeeded in leaving me with the impression that Mr Barron had not missed his children. I was, to my own surprise, unwilling to let it go at that; I wanted to go on. I wanted to find out more about Mr Barron but I was afraid of appearing unduly curious. I couldn't explain to this quiet young stranger sitting beside me that my interest was prompted solely by my feeling of affection for the two young Barrons.

So I said nothing more; I sat watching the blue sea and the blue-gray sky and thinking about Mr Barron.

Lindy finished her game and came across with Rex to join us. Neil Harper began to rise, but she shook her head and sank into a heap at my feet; Rex, with a word of excuse, went below.

'He beat me,' said Lindy, looking after him. 'Shouldn't he know, at sixteen, that it's wiser to let a woman win?'

'He'll learn,' I said.

She turned and studied Neil Harper.

'Are you glad to be going back to work,' she asked him, 'or sorry?'

'Glad.'

'Do you like Lisbon?'

'Very much.'

'Tell me about the firm,' she asked.

He hesitated.

'It flourishes,' he said at last.

'I know. But tell me about the people in it,' she said. 'I don't know anything about any of them.'

'In two days, you'll know all about them,' said Neil Harper—and smiled.

And as he did so, I saw a flicker in Lindy's eyes, and I knew what she was thinking: that the smile transformed the dark, serious face and made it almost startlingly attractive. The eyes lit with humor, the wide, mobile mouth

22

lost its sober lines. I didn't blame Lindy for staring.

With her usual frankness, she spoke out.

'Why don't you do that more often?' she asked him.

'Do what?'

'What you just did: smile. We'd begun—' Her gesture, to my embarrassment, included me. 'We'd begun to think that you couldn't, or that you didn't believe in it.'

'I'm sorry.'

'Don't be sorry; just go on smiling,' said Lindy. 'Are the people in the firm nice? I mean, do you like them?'

'If they weren't, or if I didn't, do you think that I would be likely to tell you?'

'Under the circumstances, I suppose not,' she conceded. She began to count on her fingers. 'There's my father; who comes next?'

'The two senior partners: Alec Walsh, who's English—sorry, Scottish—and a Portuguese named Senhor Luis Cunha.'

'And then there's somebody called Mr Searle. Is he older or younger than you are?'

'Older.'

'Then he's senior to you?'

'No.'

'Oh. Does he mind?'

'No, I don't think so.'

'And then there's yourself—and isn't there a new man coming out?'

'Yes. Charles Essex. He's a friend of mine,

an old school friend. In fact, I asked your father to consider taking him on in the first place.'

'Shall I like him?' Lindy asked, and Neil laughed.

'Yes; I'm sure you'll like him.'

'Aunt Kate!' Lindy turned to me in triumph. 'Are you listening? He's using long sentences! And he's smiling! And he's laughing! All he needed was sea air.' She got to her feet in a swift, graceful movement. 'Here's Rex. I can get my revenge.' She held out a hand to Neil. 'Come and play on my side,' she urged.

'Two against one?' He was on his feet, smiling down at her.

'Why not? I'm only a handicap, anyway,' she said. 'Come on.'

I didn't see her leave the cabin the following morning. When I came up on deck, I saw her walking energetically, Neil Harper by her side. Her cheeks were flushed, her eyes bright and her hair in wild disorder, and she looked as lovely as the day.

She went downstairs to find Rex and challenge him to more games, and Neil settled me in my deck chair and lowered himself in to the one next to it.

'Was that your father seeing you off at the station?' I asked him presently.

'Yes. Who was that you were wiping the platform with?' he asked with a smile.

'My brother. Was I screaming?'

24

'You were speaking perfectly quietly, but one couldn't help hearing.'

We sat in companionable silence for a time, and then I turned to him impulsively.

'Mr Harper—'

'It sounds a little overpowering,' he objected. 'If you would call me Neil—or even Theobald, to get into practice...'

'Neil, you don't like Mr Barron, do you?'

His eyebrows went up.

'What makes you—'

'I've become very fond of Lindy and Rex,' I told him earnestly. 'I like them very much, and I would like to feel that they were going to be happy with their father, and that he was ... that he was—'

'All he should be?'

'Yes.'

'Is it important?'

I stared at him.

'Of course it's important. Don't you think it is?'

'I think that girls nowadays, and boys, too, are quite well able to look after themselves,' he said quietly. 'If you asked a girl for a frank description of a good father, wouldn't she say that he was a man who signed checks when asked, and didn't interfere unless asked?'

'I think that's terribly cynical, and it's only true of one kind of girl and one kind of parent. My own son and daughter—'

I pulled myself up. This was the dangerous

25

opening. I closed my eyes and repeated my warning to myself: I must not, repeat not several times, get on to the subject of my children. Nobody, underline nobody, wants to hear anything about other people's children. Or, come to that, about me. Reticence, and dignity, and a certain quiet charm—this is for grandmothers.

I opened my eyes. Neil Harper was watching me.

'Your son and daughter?' he prompted.

'Nothing. If you had any sense, you wouldn't give me an opening like that.'

'Were you going to say that they looked up to their father?'

'They had to; he was in heaven;' I said tartly.

'But if he had been alive, you would have liked your children to be guided by him?' pursued Neil relentlessly.

'Never mind my children. We were talking about the Barrons, and you gave me the impression, I don't know quite how, that Mr Barron isn't a ... good father.'

'I have scarcely mentioned Mr Barron.'

'That's what I said. And it worried me.'

'Why?' asked Neil. 'Do you really imagine that Mr Barron will matter much to either of his children? He will provide a welcome; he'll give them a home and a good background. He's a wealthy man and a generous one, so they'll be comfortable, and they'll find their own amusements, and accept him as they find him. There's nothing worrying about that, is there?'

I said nothing. I had detected a faintly sardonic note in his voice and I felt that I had said too much already. Lindy came back with Rex and they claimed him; he rose and bowed and went off with them, and I sat on feeling that I had been about to make a fool of myself. I had taken an inordinate fancy to the two young Barrons because they reminded me of my own children, and I had been on the point of allowing my motherly instincts to lead me beyond the bounds of common sense. Tomorrow—no, the next day—they would disembark at Lisbon and after that their affairs would be no concern of mine. I would be wise to put Mr Barron and his however charming children out of my mind, and think about Sue and the baby.

But it was Neil who brought the subject up after dinner.

I had gone up on deck and had just escaped from an extremely boring woman who, seeing my name in the passenger list, had tracked me down to ask whether I knew the Verneys of Bedford, or it may have been Bradford. I got away, but she hadn't finished with me, and I pushed a deck chair to the darkest corner of the deck and sat in it, hoping to elude her. Peering over my shoulder now and then, I saw Neil in search of somebody, but I supposed it to be Lindy. Then he caught sight of me and came

27

up.

'I've been looking for you,' he said. 'What are you sitting in the gloom for?'

'I'm hiding from that woman with the toreador cloak.'

'Oh.' He brought a second chair and settled himself in it, screening me from view. 'Now, you can't be seen, and I can talk to you.'

'What about?'

'About your unusual gifts.'

'Ah, so you've noticed?'

He laughed, and then turned to me and spoke soberly.

'You gave me rather a shock today,' he said.

'How?'

'You told me that I had given you certain ideas about Mr Barron, and—'

'The trouble with me,' I broke in, 'is that I read too much into what people say. In fact—'

'In fact,' took up Neil, 'you don't listen to what they say. You hear what they don't say— and that's a very unusual gift. It's also a very disconcerting trait.'

'So there *is* something,' I said slowly, 'about Mr Barron?'

'He will enjoy having his children with him. Does that make your mind any easier?'

'To make it absolutely easy,' I said, 'you'd have to tell me that he was a thoroughly good man. But I shouldn't have asked you about him, because it was impossible for you, a member of his firm, to discuss him with

28

strangers. You were right to say nothing, and I was wrong to ask you. And if he isn't a nice man, I'd much rather not know, because I should worry all the way across the Atlantic about Lindy and Rex, and that would spoil my trip.'

'You really believe that at this late stage in their relationship, it will make much difference to the children what he is?'

'I only think that what he is, is important *for*—not *to*, but *for* his children,' I said.

'Why? Why should his way of life matter to them when they haven't set eyes on him since they were babies?'

'Because they've had a sound upbringing,' I answered. 'Their mother must have been a nice woman; those two are natural, unspoiled, and ... and decent. That doesn't come by itself—at least, I don't think it does. Decency has to grow into children, and it doesn't unless they're reared in ... in decent soil. If Lindy and Rex have been brought up by a good mother, and then go to live with a bad father, what makes you think they won't notice, or won't care?'

'Mr Barron isn't a bad man, so presumably he won't be a bad father. Please don't get the idea that there's anything wrong with him. He's an outstandingly attractive man and he's got, or he had, a weakness for pretty women, and some of the Portuguese women are very pretty indeed. If you were going to Lisbon, I'd leave you to find this out for yourself; as it is, I

29

tell you because if I don't, you'll worry. Mr Barron is an arrogant man, and doesn't take kindly to advice; there has been a scandal or two, and if he isn't careful, the authorities will get busy and the British colony will lose one of its most influential members. Try to remember that for years he has led what's virtually a bachelor existence.'

'Do you like him?'

He hesitated.

'Yes. Yes, I do, but I don't like some of the things about him: his way of walking roughshod, chiefly. I like him as a businessman, but until recently I've felt that he goes too hard after anything he wants. Recently, he's ... he's quietened down a good bit. And that's all I can say, and I hope it has set your mind at rest.'

I didn't answer. I sat there in the darkness and knew that nothing I could say would make much sense to Neil Harper. He was young, and his standards were broader than those which had existed in my own youth. You couldn't, nowadays, mention the old rules; if you did, you were told that people had outgrown them. All that old stuffiness about sex—gone, and a good thing, too, was the cry. And love was the theme, now as it always had been, but nowadays they called it sex and showed you how simple it all was once you stopped confusing it with sin. Love. Every book you picked up, almost every film you went to, almost every play your children took you to see—there were the new rules, in passionate close-ups.

'What are you thinking about?' he asked me at last.

'I'm just hoping that Lindy and Rex won't get the backwash of the scandals, that's all.'

'Isn't it all experience? Do you want their father to put up a wall between them by pretending to be something that he's not?'

'I don't want him to pretend anything. All I know is that before he can keep Lindy and Rex out of trouble, he's got to keep out of it himself. Especially that sort of trouble.'

I would, I swore to myself, forget the whole thing. And I did. I enjoyed the society of Lindy and Rex, and I put their father out of my mind. I listened to their plans; I helped Lindy to pack and I helped her to choose which dress she'd wear to land in; I said good-by to them both with affection and regret and didn't allow myself to worry about how they would get on.

When the ship docked at Lisbon, I went on deck and tried, as discreetly as possible, to get a glimpse of Mr Barron among the crowds meeting the ship. I saw a group of people who seemed to fit the descriptions Neil had given of the members of the firm—but before I could examine them individually, I heard Neil himself speaking at my elbow.

'Would you,' he asked, 'care to come ashore and let me show you around Lisbon?'

31

Surprise, for the first moment, drove out gratitude.

'But haven't you got to go and report yourself?' I asked.

'No. Every member of the firm'—he nodded towards the dock—'will be down there, waiting to greet the Big Chief's son and daughter. I've got a free day; if you'd care to look around, I'd be very glad to take you.'

'Thank you,' I said. 'I'd enjoy that very much.'

'The ship's not sailing until five-thirty. Doesn't give you much time to see any of the outlying places, but we could have a look at the city before lunch and do a couple of museums. Would that suit you?'

I said that it would suit me very well and went down to get ready, and didn't stop to tell him that I wasn't a very good person to take sight-seeing. I looked and I listened but— according to Henry—I didn't learn. A woman who'd done as much traveling as I had, said Henry, and who'd got so little intellectual benefit from it, would be hard to find. But Neil Harper needn't know that.

On my way down to the cabin, I picked up a sheaf of literature on Portugal that a thoughtful purser had placed on the tables in the lounge. Propping it up on the dressing table as I dressed, I skimmed through it, and to my surprise came across personalities I hadn't met since I left the Fifth Form all those years ago. I found myself back with Henry the Navigator, whose mother was Phillipa, daughter of John of Gaunt; old names were coming to mind: Lagos; Sagres. And then I was remembering, with even greater surprise, that Wellington had been in Portugal before I got there. Wellington, who was said to be a magnificent general, but whose strategy I had never succeeded in mastering. He had built fortifications not so very far from the cabin I was dressing in: at Torres Vedras, during the Peninsular War. The history mistress had traced the line of them on the map and I had lost the thread. Now I could go and see them, as Massena had done in 1810. There was something in history, when you came to look at it.

I came back to the present and hurried up to the deck to join Neil Harper. Before I left the cabin, I stood for a moment looking about me: the air seemed full of Lindy's delicate perfume, and the flowers she had bought me from the ship's shop stood by my bed. I wondered whether Neil had asked me out in order to take my mind off the parting, and felt more than ever grateful to him.

As we got to the bottom of the gangway, I saw Lindy and Rex standing with a group of people some distance away. I couldn't guess which of them was Mr Barron, and I didn't ask Neil to tell me. I had made my farewells and there was no point in thinking of Lindy or Rex at this moment. Neil led me to a long, low, imposing gray car; he took the wheel, and I sat beside him and as I got in, Lindy and Rex turned and saw me. I waved; they waved. Lindy blew a kiss. I waggled my fingers at her and then sat wondering what sort of fool I was to feel like crying because I was losing sight of two young people I'd met only three days ago and in all probability would never see again. I really thought, as I turned to stare at them until they were out of sight, that this was my last look at them.

Which just shows you.

CHAPTER TWO

'Won't you be rather cold in that suit?' asked Neil, as we drove away from the docks.

'I don't think so,' I said, and shivered as I spoke.

'We could easily turn back and you could get a coat.'

'No, thank you.'

It would be too humiliating to have to go back to the ship, up the gangway, down to the cabin to choose something more suitable to wear. It was cold now, but perhaps as the day advanced, it would get warmer. I was wearing a suit that the woman in the ship had assured me was the very thing for what she had called the semitropics—and I had included Lisbon in this category. But Lisbon in December is far from semitropical, and as we drove through the busy streets, I looked out and saw that everybody but myself was dressed for the semi-Arctic: men were wearing short, thick coats with fur collars, peasant women were swathed in shawls, and in the shiny, immensely long American cars that flashed by, I caught glimpses of women in fur coats. I hoped for a moment that Neil would insist on going back to the ship, but he was making plans as to how we should spend the day.

'There isn't time to get out to Sagres and back,' he said. 'How about Torres Vedras?'

'You mean all those ditches and things?'

'If you call them ditches. They're the old fortifications, and they're interesting.'

'Some other time.'

We had left the main roads with the yellow trams, and we were driving up narrow, twisting streets where sheets and shirts hung drying on lines slung high across the road. I felt like Queen Victoria on Jubilee Day, driving through beflagged streets in the poorer quarters of London. But the houses in London weren't painted pale pink and violent blue, like the ones we were passing; they didn't have balconies overhung with flowers; donkeys didn't slip and slither past the car. And in London, there were no palm trees, and the streets didn't have names like Concepcaõ, or

Misericordia, or Fieis de Deus.

I should have known better than to go sight-seeing with a man, and a young, strong man at that. My hints about looking at the shops were wasted; my reference to midmorning coffee was ignored. Other women sat at ease, sipping this and that, while I walked with my escort around Black Horse Square and gazed at the statue of Dom Pedro IV. I tried to look interested and succeeded so well that Neil took me to see the statues of the Marquis of Pombal, and d'Almeida Garrett, and Castilho. Then, running out of statues, he took me to the Museum of Ancient Art. Then we went to the Museum of Contemporary Art and on to the Military Museum (Peninsular War on the first floor). My feet were throbbing and my head was spinning, and when we got out onto the street, a cold wind was waiting to whistle straight through my new suit and out the other side.

'Would you like to go back and put on a warmer suit now, or after lunch?' inquired Neil, his eyes fixed on the road.

I gave in. 'Now, please,' I said.

He turned the car.

'I'll drive you to the office and I'll pick up a chauffeur and send you back while I collect my letters from the office. He'll bring you to the restaurant,' said Neil.

I was driven back to the ship. The jetty was cold, and I hurried across the space between

36

the car and the gangway. I had my foot on the bottom step when I heard Lindy's voice.

'Wait—oh, please wait!'

I turned. She was running towards me. Rex was coming out from the shadow of a shed. I stepped off the gangway and waited for them.

'I—We were looking for you,' Lindy said, as she came up to me.

She sounded breathless, but it wasn't because she had been running.

'Is anything the matter?' I asked.

'I don't know. My—' She hesitated, and it was Rex who finished the sentence.

'It's just—My father isn't—He didn't come.'

There was a pause. I thought of a hundred reasons why Mr Barron had failed to meet the boat. As fast as the reasons came, I rejected them.

'But I saw you as I drove away,' I said at last. 'There were a great many people—'

'Yes. But my father wasn't among them.'

We looked at one another. They seemed to think that I ought to say something.

'Why are you alone here now?' I asked.

'We went home,' said Rex. 'To my father's house. But he wasn't there. He hadn't been there since very early this morning.'

There was another pause.

'But ... you mean nobody knew where he was?' I asked.

'They all came to meet us, thinking he'd be here,' explained Lindy. 'But he wasn't. The

37

office people were all here—there was Senhor Cunha, and his wife, and Mr Walsh, and Mr Searle. We all waited and waited, and then they telephoned, and Mr Searle went off to look, and then we were taken to the house, and the servants said that he wasn't there and hadn't been there since he went out for his usual early morning ride.'

'But ... but didn't anybody know where—'

'They said he'd gone out about seven in the morning. He didn't come back.'

'But—the office?'

'He hadn't been there.'

'But who's at the house now?' I asked. 'Didn't anybody stay with you?'

'They were coming back,' said Rex. 'They went to ... to make inquiries and to ... to look in the places my father rides in. They told us not to worry.'

'That was a silly thing to tell you,' I said. 'Why did you come back to the ship? Did you think your father—'

'We wanted to find you,' said Lindy.

It was a fatal thing to say. To me, I mean. You can ask some people for help and they give it to you within their capacity. You ask others and they confess, reluctantly, that they can't do anything. You ask someone else—me, for example—and I know with absolute certainty that I can do nothing, but when I try to say so, the words won't come. What comes is a stream of completely convincing sentences of

38

reassurance, of comfort and of hope. I can hear myself now; I sounded calm and serene and in complete control of the situation, and I could see the color coming back into Lindy's cheeks and the strained look leaving her brother's eyes—and I didn't know the first thing about who was going to do what next.

When I'd finished speaking, everything had been smoothed out: Mr Barron had been delayed and only those idiots at the office could have forgotten what he'd told them about why and how. All this unnecessary worry—and for what? Pooh.

Lindy gave a deep sigh.

'I'm so glad you weren't lunching out,' she said. 'I prayed.'

Her prayer was answered. I wasn't lunching out.

'But my goodness,' I said, 'I forgot to tell the chauffeur that I wouldn't need him any more. Just a moment.'

I went over to the car and began to explain that I was desolated, but would he please explain to Mr Harper that I had been taken ill and thanks anyway? The chauffeur, however, had not one word of English, and I remembered that Neil had produced, when speaking to him, an impressive flow of Portuguese. I resorted to mime; it wasn't graceful, but it was effective; the chauffeur nodded, bowed, removed his peaked hat politely, put it on again and drove away. I watched him go out of sight and hoped that Neil would know that I was grateful for the lunch I hadn't had. He would know why I hadn't come; when he went to the office, he would be told the news.

I went back to Lindy and Rex.

'Come on board with me a few moments,' I said. 'I've got to get into something warmer. Then I'll go back to the house with you and give your father a piece of my mind for keeping you waiting.'

I put on a warm suit, and Rex and Lindy sat on my bed as I finished doing my hair and told me as much as they knew about their new home. It was large—very large, they said—and there were five servants and a great many bathrooms and an outdated kitchen with an archaic wood-burning stove. There was a lovely view of the estuary. There was a drawing room in which forty couples could dance. There were colored tiles half the way up the walls of every room. It was all wonderful—or it would be when Father got home.

We drove there in a cramped taxi; to get into a Lisbon taxi, you have to have a slender body and no legs. We climbed narrow and twisting streets, as I had done with Neil Harper earlier that morning, and then we found ourselves high up on a quiet street, driving towards a beautiful wrought-iron gateway. We entered and stopped before an imposing house painted a cool gray; on one of the walls, in blue and white tiles, was its name: *Casa Roma*.

'This is it,' said Rex. 'Look, we'll pay the taxi.'

'Look, you won't,' I said. 'To save hard feelings, we'll share it.'

We halved it and then we walked up a broad flight of steps to the front door. Rex pushed an electric bell and I waited for one of the five servants to answer the summons. But when the door opened, I saw a tall, fair, well-built man of about thirty-six standing before us. At the sight of Lindy and Rex, he gave an exclamation of relief and threw the door open to its widest extent.

'I was worried about you both,' he said. 'Where did you go off to?'

'We went to look for Mrs Verney,' Lindy told him. 'We—She's a friend of ours and she came back with us to see if my father was here. Mrs Verney, this is Mr Searle—he's in Daddy's firm.'

Mr Searle ushered us into the drawing room, and I turned to him and spoke the words I knew Lindy and Rex were afraid to utter.

'Is there any news of Mr Barron?'

'No news yet, I'm afraid,' said Mr Searle. 'But we all know—' he gave us a wide, all-too-reassuring smile—'we all know that no news is good news.'

Nobody answered. It was clear to me, and I think to Lindy and Rex, too, that he thought the lack of news far from good.

41

'There's a thorough search going on,' he told us. 'I've been out, and so has Mr Walsh; the Cunhas are riding over the route Mr Barron usually takes, and of course, the police are—'

'The police ...' breathed Lindy.

'They had to be informed,' Mr Searle told her. 'It's not because we fear anything ... serious; it's just a routine matter. Mr Walsh thought that they ought to be told.'

'Mr Searle.' It was Rex speaking; the older man turned to him reluctantly, and I could see that he was dreading questions.

'Well, Rex?'

'When we were in the house an hour ago, there were a lot of servants, but I didn't see any sign of them when we came in just now. There was a sort of houseboy, and—'

Lindy rose from the low chair on which she had been seated.

'Could we go and look?' she asked.

'Of course,' said Mr Searle.

She went out with Rex. As the door closed behind them, Mr Searle's eyes met mine, and I saw in his, without restraint or concealment, all the feelings that he had been keeping back. He looked white and drawn—and frightened. The fear in his eyes struck a chill through me, because he did not appear to be a man who would be easily frightened; there was something about him that made me feel that he had as a rule almost too much confidence—a confidence amounting to recklessness.

42

'They won't find any servants,' he told me in a low, hurried voice. 'They've gone.'

'Gone?' I echoed stupidly. 'Gone where?'

'Disappeared. The police came here and questioned them. I don't know what they wanted to find out, but they put the fear of God into them and they ... faded away.'

'All of them?'

'All except one: Zulmyra, the cook.'

'You mean that they won't come back?'

'That depends on what has happened to Mr Barron. If he's safe, if he's found and brought back and it turns out to have been an accident, they'll come back. If there's any fear of ... of further questioning, I think they'll make themselves rather difficult to locate. They don't like getting mixed up unless they have to.'

'Mixed up in what?'

'In—'

'You've got news of some kind,' I said. 'What is it?'

'You won't tell Miss Barron and her brother?'

'No. But they'll have to know eventually, you must realize. What have you heard?'

'They found Mr Barron's horse. It was at the bottom of a steep slope—dead. It had fallen from a narrow path, a sort of steep ledge high up on the side of a hill.'

'And ... and Mr Barron?'

'No sign. That's where they are now—

looking. But until they find something, there's no need—'

No need. No need for those two to know that they had come to a house of tragedy. No need for them to learn the worst, with its ghastly details. No need...

I pulled myself up sharply, ashamed of my momentary conviction that Mr Barron was dead. I looked at Mr Searle.

'Where is this place?' I asked.

'Mr Barron's horses are stabled here, but he owns a piece of rough ground about three or four miles outside Lisbon, and he does most of his riding there. He goes out every morning without fail. The groom rides the horse out there and back again; Mr Barron goes there and returns by car. The path that the horse fell from ... nobody but Mr Barron ever uses it. It's too dangerous; it's a hair-raising drop, but he's a magnificent horseman and he goes along the path every morning and thinks nothing of it. Today, perhaps—'

'But the groom?'

'Hasn't come back either. And Mr Barron's car can't be found.'

'But if Mr Barron fell over the edge, it must be easy to—'

'To find him? No. Those slopes are thickly wooded. They'd have to cut their way—'

He stopped. Lindy and Rex were crossing the hall.

'They've gone,' Lindy told us as they entered

44

the room. 'All except Zulmyra. She says, as far as I can make out, that the ... police frightened them.'

'That's what I suspected; I've just been telling Mrs Verney so.' Mr Searle's voice was firmer than it had been. 'I wouldn't worry much, Miss Barron. When your father gets back, so will they. Would you like me to talk to Zulmyra?'

Before she could reply, there was an interruption. The front doorbell had rung, and Rex went to answer it. He returned with two people—a man and a woman—and I understood from Lindy's greeting that she had met them on the dock that morning. She brought them up to me and I learned that they were Senhor Cunha and his wife.

Senhor Cunha was not engaging; he was short, stout, middle-aged and far from handsome—but his wife made me wish that one were permitted to rest one's eyes as long and as openly upon beautiful people as one could upon beautiful scenes. Nature had never created anything lovelier than Sylvana Cunha, but all that good manners allowed me was a glance whenever I thought myself unobserved.

She was not more than twenty, and incredibly tiny; her waist, her hands and feet were so small that they looked like a child's. Her face was oval and her eyes black velvet. I knew that Henry, after a brief survey, would say that in ten years time she would be stout and coarse and look twice her age, but I didn't think so. She wouldn't always, of course, have this ethereal quality, but her eyes would still be beautiful, her hair still soft and blue-black, her skin perhaps as dazzling. If Mr Barron liked Portuguese beauties—and Neil Harper had said that he did—here was one very close to hand.

Both the Cunhas were in riding clothes. They took little notice of me, but their brief glance shattered instantly any illusions I might have had about being a support to Lindy and Rex; both husband and wife, without saying a word, made it clear that in their view I would have done better to refrain from intruding at a time like this.

They made their report—for what they had to say was in the nature of a report. Sitting there, unregarded, on the long, modern sofa, I got a clearer picture of the morning's events. The senior partners of the firm of Barron and Walsh—Alec Walsh and Senhor Cunha—had gone that morning to meet the *Juan Cortez*. With them had been Senhora Cunha and Mr Searle. The fact that the head of the firm was not there to meet his children occasioned, for a time, no comment and no uneasiness. But the ship had docked, the passengers had begun to disembark and still there was no sign of Mr Barron. After waiting, after telephoning to the house and to the office, after making a series of dashes to places in which Mr Barron was likely

46

to be found, they had all presented as reassuring a front as possible to Mr Barron's son and daughter. They had brought them to the house, and then the Cunhas had gone away to change into riding clothes and had ridden over the country that Mr Barron usually covered on his rides. Mr Walsh had gone to the office and from there had summoned the police. The police had come to the house and questioned the servants, and it was about this time that Lindy and Rex had gone back to the ship in the hope of finding me. Out of the morning's bewilderment and confusion, the most likely conclusion had been reached and was being acted upon: Mr Barron had met with a riding accident. He would be found by his friends or by the police. He would be brought home and nursed back to health.

It was all very thin. Lindy and Rex listened to the expressions of hope and encouragement and said nothing, but the shadows in their eyes grew deeper. For myself, I was fighting off a feeling that there was something in the attitude of Mr Searle and the Cunhas, something hidden, something fearful and tense, that could not be explained. There was something more than anxiety in our midst. There was fear, and it was fear that went beyond the thought of a possible spill from a horse. The members of the firm had reason to be worried, or pitying or apprehensive; they might recoil from the thought that these two young people had come out full of hope, and had come too late. All these emotions were right and natural, but they were feeling something more: fear, and a sort of horror.

It was then, I think, that I had my first impulse to get away. I wanted to go back to the ship and stay on it. I might tell myself that the impulse was unworthy; I might tell myself that the excitement of the journey had overheated my imagination. I did all this, and my conviction remained unchanged: there was danger somewhere near.

I was to feel moments of panic later, again and again, but when they came, they brought the knowledge that I was in this thing and had to stay in it to the end. But I wasn't in it—yet. At that moment, I wasn't deeply involved, and all my strongest instincts urged me to escape. My place, I told myself, was not here with this little Portuguese man and his exquisite wife and with this unstable-looking man called Searle. And if Henry could see me now, he would say that I had brought it all on myself.

But even at this stage, withdrawal would have been impossible. Lindy and Rex listened to the others, and looked at me. I was nothing to them, and the other people in the room were their father's associates—but they were looking at me and waiting for me to say something.

My first contribution to the conversation wasn't notable, but it was effective.

'I'm terribly hungry,' I said.

There was an instant's blank pause while Mr Searle and the two Cunhas turned to stare at me—and then the three of them broke into animated speech and I understood that in that moment they had suddenly, and with enormous relief, seen the possibility of my usefulness. I was no longer an intrusive outsider; I was—Why, I could see them asking themselves, hadn't they thought of it before? I was a diversion, an indispensable ally. I could stay with Lindy and Rex during these hours of suspense, and relieve the members of Mr Barron's firm of much worry and embarrassment. I could translate harsh realities into suitably soft terms for his children; I could engage their attention and prevent them from putting unanswerable questions about the events of the morning.

Senhor Cunha had spread out his hands and was talking in a tone of mingled regret and apology. But of course, I had made him aware ... yes, it was unpardonable that he should have forgotten what was due ... lunch ... food ... drink ... inexcusable remissness.

It took some time to make a sensible plan; Mr Searle made suggestions, and the Cunhas brushed them aside and made fresh ones, but at last it was arranged that I should go with Lindy and Rex to lunch at the Negresco; the Cunhas would go home and change and meet us there; we would be driven there eventually in Mr

Searle's car. And in the meantime, the house was of course Miss Barron's; she must make herself at home.

We all walked across the hall and stood on the steps and watched the Cunhas drive away in their large and expensive car. Mr Searle left—to pay a quick visit to the office, he told us—immediately afterwards. Lindy and Rex and I turned and went back into the house.

'I think I should change,' said Lindy.

'I'd like to, too,' said Rex. 'Will you take Aunt Kate up?'

We went up the graceful, curving staircase and walked along a wide corridor; Rex disappeared into a room at the end, and Lindy opened a door halfway down and ushered me into a large, sunny room.

I went inside and walked slowly forward, taking in details as I went, and I saw that if fate had robbed Mr Barron of the opportunity to welcome his daughter in person, this room would do much to make her understand how much he had looked forward to her coming. Everywhere were touches, some of them only too clearly a man's, which showed tenderness and affection. Flowers, books; on the bed, a heap of prettily wrapped packages, clearly presents. There was a photograph of a woman on the dressing table, and I stopped to look at it. Lindy came and stood at my shoulder.

'My mother,' she said.

I stared at the likeness.

'It's a pity ...' I said at last.

'Yes. She told me,' said Lindy, 'that she would have agreed to a divorce if he had asked for one. But he never asked.'

I turned to look at her.

'Do you feel that you know him at all?' I asked.

She hesitated.

'Until I came into this room ... no,' she said at last. 'I expected a lot; I mean that I expected too much, because I thought, when we were on our way out here, that I would be able to visualize him, see him as a real father. But I couldn't. It wasn't until I walked into this room this morning that it ... that I seemed to see him clearly.' A dreadful whiteness overspread her cheeks and she made a clutch at my hand. 'Aunt Kate, do you think it's ... too late?'

'No.' I was astonished at the promptness and firmness of my answer. 'No. It isn't too late, Lindy. Even if he's badly hurt, or—' I hesitated and then brought the word out steadily—'or dead, it isn't too late. He tried to say something, in this room, of how much he was looking forward to seeing you and to having you here. It isn't too late to understand that he loved you.'

As I spoke, I was trying to reconcile this Mr Barron with the other: the William Barron who pursued pretty women, who had been involved in scandals, who had made enemies and who

51

was now missing. There were two William Barrons, and I would have liked to know which was the real one, but it was probable that when they found him, dead or alive, I would be on the *Juan Cortez*, on my way across the Atlantic, with my thoughts pretty well equally divided between Lindy and Rex here in Lisbon, and Sue and my grandson in South America.

While Lindy changed, I washed in her bathroom and combed my hair and made up my face. As she was still not quite ready, I asked if I might wander around and look at the house.

'Of course, go anywhere you like,' she said. 'I'll meet you down in the drawing room in a few minutes.'

I walked slowly around the upper part of the house. Henry would have been interested in the rugs and the furniture, but I was enchanted by the lovely view to be seen from every window. A lovely home, I thought; a home that Lindy and Rex could be happy in ... if their father ever came back to share it.

I went downstairs. There was not a sound in the house. I found the silence eerie and wished that I could have heard my own footsteps making loud and companionable noises on the stairs, but my shoes had the thin rubber soles and heels which I always have put on them when they're new, and which Henry, without any idea of being funny, calls my sole saving. I reached the hall feeling a little depressed; the desertion of the servants had given the place a haunted look, I thought.

I stood looking around the hall. Several doors led off it; one of them I knew to be that of the drawing room. The one opposite looked as though it might lead to the dining room. I walked to it and opened it, and as I did so, I found that Lindy had come downstairs, unheard, and was at my elbow.

To this day, I don't know why I opened the door so quietly. I think it was the effect of the silence and the emptiness and the loneliness of the house. At all events, I took hold of the handle—it was a handle and not a knob—and pushed it down and opened the door soundlessly at the same moment that I became aware of Lindy beside me.

We stood there for a moment, looking in, and then I shut the door as quietly as I had opened it. But this time there was no question of why I did so. I strained every nerve to prevent myself from making a sound.

Then Lindy and I stood outside the room, listening. If the woman in there had heard us, surely she would come out? But there was no movement except the rustle of papers. I could see Lindy's face of blank wonder; I could hear my heart thumping. As we stood there, silent and unmoving, my thoughts raced, but I couldn't reach any conclusion as to why the lovely Sylvana Cunha was in Mr Barron's study, bending over his desk and searching feverishly among his papers.

For the search had been feverish. Frenzied. And it had been furtive. She was looking for something, and whatever it was, she was desperately anxious to find it—and I knew from the combination of haste and caution with which she was searching that she did not intend anybody to know that the papers had been disturbed.

I stood there with Lindy, trying to find a reason for the caution, and then gave it up. Then I saw that Lindy had gone to the foot of the stairs and was calling up to Rex, for the purpose, as her glance showed me, of making our presence known to the woman in the study.

'Rex!' she called. 'Hurry up—I'm hungry!'

We waited, but we weren't waiting for an answer from Rex. We were listening for other sounds. But there was silence; there was not even the rustle of papers. Then we heard the sound of a car, and the scrunching of wheels on the gravel of the drive. Through the window of the hall we could see a car going out of the gate. It was Mr Searle's, and there were two people in it: Mr Searle and Sylvana Cunha.

Lindy and I turned and walked into the study. The window was open; I walked to it and looked out and saw the wheel marks of a car on the drive; it took no great acumen to conclude that Sylvana Cunha, who had driven away with her husband to change for lunch, had returned, still unchanged, had looked for something among Mr Barron's papers, had climbed out of the long window and had driven away with Robert Searle.

It didn't make much sense to either of us, but we didn't try to work it out; we could stand there asking one another questions, but neither of us could supply any answers. I had been aware, in the drawing room before the Cunhas and Mr Searle went away, that there was more to Mr Barron's disappearance than people were prepared to divulge. I would, perhaps, know all the answers one day. Lindy would write to me and tell me what had happened; she would, perhaps, explain why Sylvana Cunha went out one way with her husband and came back another way with Robert Searle. I would learn what she had been looking for among Mr Barron's papers.

I wondered whether Mr Barron had been paying too much attention to the exquisite Sylvana; had her husband, I wondered, written an incriminating letter to Mr Barron? Did Sylvana know this, and was she looking for the letter?

I didn't think so. From what I had seen of the Senhora and her cool bearing towards her husband, I felt that she would be more concerned with planting than with suppressing evidence that would incriminate him. And Robert Searle? Where did he fit in? And the servants? Was the routine questioning by the police enough to frighten them, or did they know something that they did not wish to tell the police?

I had no idea. I could only stand beside Lindy and listen to her questions and shake my head. We must have been deeply absorbed, for when at last we came out of our mood of useless speculation, I saw Lindy glance at her watch and heard her soft exclamation of surprise.

'I'll go up and call Rex,' she said.

She went upstairs, and I walked slowly towards the drawing room. I had heard no sounds of any arrivals, and I expected to find the room empty as we had left it.

But when I opened the door and went in, I forgot Luis Cunha and his wife Sylvana; I forgot Robert Searle. I even forgot Mr Barron and his children for some moments. I stood on the threshold staring in open admiration at the woman inside.

And so would anybody have done, on getting their first view of Athena Rodrigues.

CHAPTER THREE

I shut the door of the drawing room behind me and tried to sort out my sensations. When I had looked at little Senhora Cunha, I had felt admiration but no envy—but now envy was filling me. Sylvana Cunha was young and slim

56

and lovely, and all I had felt on looking at her was a detached pleasure—but the woman standing at the table helping herself to a liberal drink was neither young nor slim. She was of middle height, like me; she was no longer young—me again—but she was a picture of elegance, and it was because of this that I envied her. She had, I saw at that first glance, no more original claim to beauty than I had, but she gave an impression of good looks. She had a finish, a polish that took my breath away.

She was the first to speak.

'Who're you?' she asked casually.

'My name's Verney. Mrs Verney. I'm a friend of Lindy and Rex Barron.'

'You live in Lisbon?'

'No. I'm traveling to South America on the *Juan Cortez*, the ship that came in this morning.'

'Staying long?'

'In Lisbon? No. The ship sails at half past five.'

'I'm Athena Rodrigues,' she told me. 'English by birth, Portuguese by marriage. I'm a widow. Are you?'

'Yes.'

She lifted her glass in salute. 'Wonderful state, isn't it? No woman should want to be anything else. We've got all the status and none of the setbacks. Don't you agree?'

'In a way,' I said guardedly.

'I belong, in a way, to the firm of Barron and

57

Walsh. I inherited my husband's interest in it. I suppose you've heard that Barron is missing?'

'Yes.'

'I didn't go down to meet the ship. That was a staff affair; I don't have to bother with all that. I was going to drop in during the morning to see the girl and boy—can't remember their names for the moment.'

'Lindy and Rex.'

'That's it. Melinda and Kingswell. Neil Harper was on the ship too, wasn't he?'

'Yes.'

'I was going to come in and take a look at them, and then Alec Walsh rang me up and told me that Bill Barron was missing and said he'd meet me here. Hasn't he arrived yet?'

'Mr Walsh? No. Mr Searle was here, and the Cunhas.'

'Where've they gone?'

'They went to change—they're giving us lunch; Mr Searle is driving us to the Negresco to meet them.'

'I see. Drink?' inquired Athena.

'No, thanks. Lindy and Rex ought to be down in a moment.'

We were both standing; now Athena lowered herself into a chair, crossed her legs and looked up at me, glass in hand. I looked down at her, taking in this and that. We were so much alike—and so amazingly different. I was as God and time had made me, and now I regretted it. Athena was a woman who

58

obviously watched every move that time was preparing to make, and forestalled it. Her hair, her skin, her figure—I could see exactly how much care had been taken with them. Pages from fashion magazines sprang out at me and reproached me. I had looked at them; Athena could have posed for them. I looked at her sleek perfection and I felt terrible. I felt mousy and ill-dressed and awkward. And she saw that I did.

'Have you known Lindy and Rex long?' she asked.

'No. Only since we left England. But you can get to know people very well,' I found myself adding defensively, 'on board ship.'

I heard Athena's hoarse chuckle. 'Don't tell me; I've traveled. Did you say you were going off at half past five?'

'Yes. I wouldn't be here now if Lindy and Rex hadn't come to me when they heard that their father was missing.'

'You mean they went back to fetch you?'

'Yes. I think they felt that I was the only person they knew well—at least, they know I'm fond of them.'

'How are they taking all this?'

I frowned. 'There's nothing to take—yet. They're waiting, that's all. I feel desperately sorry for them.'

'It's a pity you're not staying. They'll need someone.'

I stared down at her.

'You mean ... you mean that there's no hope of their father—'

'I mean that I think there's going to be trouble.'

'There's trouble now. Do you mean you think this is more than an accident?'

'Bill Barron,' she said slowly, 'is one of the finest riders you can see anywhere in the world. We all know that, and I for one don't believe he fell off that ledge. He's ridden along it—against everybody's advice—every morning for years; so have the three horses he owns; it isn't as if he'd been schooling a new one. And if he fell, why haven't they found him?'

'Mr Searle said the country was—'

'Rough; yes—but there's been plenty of time to find Barron.'

'If you don't think he met with a riding accident, what do you ... what do you think has happened to him?'

'William Barron,' she said, 'is a man who has spent the last few years asking for trouble. People like that find it, sooner or later. Did the police come to the house?'

'Yes. They questioned the servants and—'

'I suppose they decamped? I thought so; I had to let myself in just now.'

'There's one left—Zulmyra.'

'Deaf as a post—that's why the police couldn't scare her. It makes it awkward for Lindy and Rex; they can't stay here without servants. Some arrangement will have to be

60

made for them until their father's found—or until they have to be shipped home again,' said Athena.

I thought of Lindy and Rex on a ship— going back. Not going home. Perhaps my feelings showed on my face; at any rate, when Athena spoke again, it was in a softer tone.

'They couldn't stay here without servants,' she said. 'They may be used to doing for themselves in England, but they weren't in a house of this size and they didn't have to deal with wood stoves. They couldn't hope to run this place.'

'No, I suppose not. But—'

'I wouldn't worry too much, you know. Things may turn out all right.' She finished her drink, got up and poured herself another and sat down again. 'Bill's always been pretty good at taking care of himself; if it comes to trouble, you can rest assured that he'll give as much as he gets, Mrs—'

'Verney.'

'I can't bear formality. What's the rest of it?'

'Kate.'

'*Kate?*'

'Well, Katrina—but everybody calls me Kate.'

'Then you should stop them at once. You don't suppose Athena's my real name, do you? Nothing real about me, I'm proud to say. If I were real, I'd look just like—'

She stopped, a little too late; it was obvious

that she had been about to say 'like you.' If there was any awkwardness in the moment, however, it was only on my part; Athena was frowning over a new thought.

'It must have been obvious to you,' she said, 'that Searle and the Cunhas weren't just expecting to hear that Barron fell over the ledge and couldn't be found. Don't you know anything about William Barron?'

'No.'

'Well, he likes danger, and he likes women—and in this country the combination isn't healthy. There are lots of things that could have happened to Bill, and falling over a cliff is the nicest of them all. If it'll make you any happier, I can tell you that nothing will touch Lindy or Rex. If the police find out anything, I'll see that we all concoct a story and keep the two of them away from any real unpleasantness. But it's a pity they ever came out here. You needn't look like that. My own guess is that Bill may turn out to be all right after all. There's more than a possibility that he may have skipped out.'

'Skipped out?' I echoed stupidly.

'Yes. He's had a number of threatening letters in his time.'

'But—'

'Perhaps, this time, the threats were directed against his children. In that case, he'd have to move, and move fast. But that doesn't account for the death of the horse.'

The room seemed to go slowly around and settle again. I thought of Lindy in our cabin, dressing, undressing, brushing her teeth, taking a shower and coming out with a towel draped carelessly around her lovely young body. I saw her on deck with Rex, walking and laughing as the ship threw them off balance. I saw the open sea and felt the strong, fresh breeze. That, for the past three days. And now ... a missing man and threatening letters. A woman bending over a desk in the study, and a man waiting outside. I saw the dark, unreadable Cunha—and this woman facing me, drink in hand, groomed and elegant and speaking in a careless, casual tone of matters that to me were filled with dread. There was nothing here for Lindy and Rex of gentleness or sympathy or kindly protection. Lindy and Rex...

I heard Athena's voice.

'There's the doorbell,' she said. 'Must be Alec. Zulmyra won't hear anything.'

She made no move to answer the bell; one of her shoes was off and she was gently kneading her foot. In spite of my conviction that it was her place to go, and not mine, I found myself crossing the hall and opening the front door.

A man was standing with his back to me, looking towards the road. For a few seconds before he turned, I thought he was Robert Searle; height, breadth, set of the head were all Searle's—and then he turned and I saw that he wasn't Searle. He was every middle-aged woman's dream: he was tall and graying, lean, spruce, handsome, attractive—well, he was Alec Walsh.

My pleasure must have shown clearly on my face, but I wasn't looking pleased because he was handsome. I was feeling almost weak with relief, because here at last, I felt, was someone with whom I could leave Lindy and Rex; someone who seemed to me calm and dependable, strong and reliable; a man who looked, in his own way, as upright as Henry. I felt certain that he wouldn't be heartless, like Athena; he wouldn't be furtive, like Sylvana or Searle; he had none of Senhor Cunha's secretiveness.

Looking back, I think that what I really felt at that moment was what's called the charm of familiarity. I knew where I was; confronting me was something seen more often in advertisements than in real life: the typical English gentleman. And whatever other nations have to say about him, nobody will deny that he looks thoroughly reliable. Unshakeable. The mere sight of him was a tonic. I opened the door wide.

'Please come in,' I said. 'You're Mr Walsh.'

'Yes. Is—'

'Mrs Rodrigues is in the drawing room. All the servants—except one—have gone.'

He came in and shut the door, and stood for a moment looking down at me questioningly. I

64

would have explained who I was, but Athena, from the door of the drawing room, did it for me; her drink was in her hand and she sounded mocking.

'Mrs Verney, Alexander Walsh,' she said. 'Alec, Mrs Verney is a friend of Lindy and Rex, but she's got to go off at five-thirty.'

'Go where to?' Mr Walsh asked me.

'I'm on the *Juan Cortez*, sailing this evening.'

He walked with me towards the drawing room and I told him that Lindy and Rex would be down soon. Even as I spoke, we heard them on the stairs and Alec went to the foot of the staircase to meet them.

'Good-looking, eh?' said Athena to me under her breath.

I knew she meant Alec Walsh, but I pretended to misunderstand.

'They're a nice pair,' I said.

Alec brought them into the drawing room and introduced them to Athena. She nodded casually to Rex and then let her eyes rest for a long moment on Lindy—a cool look, neither friendly nor unfriendly, frankly speculative— then she turned at the sound of Alec Walsh's voice.

'What's been arranged about lunch?' he asked.

I told him, and he looked at Athena.

'It would be better, perhaps,' he said, 'if I took Mrs Verney and Lindy and Rex to lunch and you joined the Cunhas.'

'Nothing doing,' said Athena promptly. 'I don't like them, for one thing. They don't like me, for another. And I don't like having to talk Portuguese all the time, as they insist on doing when they're with me. No, thank you; no Cunhas.'

Rex gave her a half-smile; I felt that he had not been favorably impressed by Senhor Cunha and his wife. I wanted, suddenly, to go across to Lindy and urge her to tell Alec Walsh about the scene in the study—but there was no time and no opportunity; the doorbell had rung once more, and Robert Searle was waiting to drive us to the Negresco.

I don't remember anything about the lunch. We ate, I suppose, and drank, but all I could think of was the look on Lindy's face as the time went by and brought the sailing time of the ship nearer. We weren't allowed to forget; we met some fellow passengers on our way into lunch and ran into another group on our way out. Driving back to Mr Barron's house we passed a taxi piled high with luggage for the *Juan Cortez*.

When we got to the house, the Cunhas left us; we went in and found Alec Walsh and Athena inside. With them, to my relief and pleasure, was Neil Harper.

Some of my depression left me. He looked like an old, old friend, and I greeted him like one and remembered that when I left he would be here to watch over Lindy and Rex. That he would be a support to them, I had not the slightest doubt; looking at Lindy and Rex as they greeted him, I knew that they felt as I did.

He said little; Alec Walsh was talking, and we learned from what he told us that he had been to the police and found that there was still no news of Mr Barron. We all took this calmly; we had, I think, given up hope of hearing good news, and were bracing ourselves to hear the worst. But when the subject of Lindy and Rex came up, there was an unexpected complication. Both of them refused, quietly but positively, to move out of the house while awaiting news of their father. They were prepared, if necessary, to engage new servants; they would even live here without servants; they would, however, remain in the house, live there, sleep there until there was news—of whatever kind.

'We can manage,' said Lindy. 'We're used to doing things for ourselves and we're not children. We don't mind being alone. But we feel that we must stay in the house.'

'If you want to stay, you shall,' Alec promised them, and I felt my heart going out to him in gratitude. 'Neil will find servants for you; if Zulmyra goes off like the others, it won't matter; Neil will see to it that there's someone here to look after you. But the probability is that your own servants will come back. And now,' he added, 'Neil and I had better get back to the office. I'll come at once and tell you when we get any news.'

He went away, and Athena went with him, but Neil lingered for a moment as he passed Lindy, and stood looking down at her with a slight frown.

'If you want me,' he said, 'I'll come at any time. You can ring me at the office or—' he took out his wallet and extracted a card—'at this address: my flat. And—' He smiled; a brief but infinitely reassuring smile. 'Shall I tell you something? Everything's going to be all right.'

Lindy looked up at him, and I saw tears film her eyes.

'Thank you,' she said shakily. 'I ... I hope so.'

He took one of her hands into his strong ones and held it for a moment—and then he had followed the others, and we were alone. And as soon as the door closed behind him, Lindy walked to the window and stood staring out unseeingly, while tears trickled slowly down her cheeks.

I was, on the whole, glad. Suspense is hard to bear, and she had shown a great deal of courage; crying would do her no harm. I took her hand and patted it, but said nothing. Rex lay on the sofa, his feet up, hands behind his head, brooding. The minutes ticked by, and presently Lindy wiped her eyes, blew her nose forlornly and looked at me.

'I wish you weren't going,' she said.

'So do I, Lindy. But I must. If I thought that

I could do anything by staying,' I said, 'I'd stay. But you have friends here, and I can leave you safely in Neil's hands. And in Mr Walsh's.'

I didn't mention the other members of the firm, for I knew that Lindy and Rex, like myself, placed no faith in them whatsoever. I longed to stay. If I had been a friend of long standing, I would unhesitatingly have sent a cable to Sue and stayed in Lisbon until Lindy and Rex had no further need of me. But I wasn't a friend of long standing. I was merely a woman these two had met on board and taken a fancy to. Nobody knew me; nobody knew anything about me. I had no status. If I stayed, I would appear to everybody an interloper. Everybody but Neil, I added to myself.

'What I'd like more than anything,' said Rex suddenly, 'is a walk.'

The words, coming out of the heavy silence, had a tonic effect.

'I'd like one, too,' I said. 'In fact, I think it's what we all need. Lindy, will you come?'

'I'd love to.'

We went. We walked up and down steep streets and looked at the infinite variety of the houses we passed: every color, every style. We climbed until we got to a point from which we could see the city spread at our feet; we gazed over the roof tops to the blue waters of the estuary. I could see, far below, the funnels of the *Juan Cortez* and remembered that in an hour or two I would be making my way to the

69

vessel. By nightfall, I would be far out to sea, leaving Lisbon and Lindy and Rex behind.

I made up my mind that they must not come to see me off. I would go quickly and suddenly, before they realized that I was leaving.

'What I'd like more than anything in the world,' I said, when we had walked, I thought, a hundred miles, 'is a nice cup of tea.'

They laughed. It was good to hear them.

'Ice cream for me,' said Rex. 'But I don't see anything that looks like a café anywhere here.'

'I only know one word of Portuguese,' I told them, 'and it's *cha*. Any place that says *cha* will provide tea.'

Most of the places in the vicinity that had *cha* painted on their signs, however, looked far from inviting. We went on until we came to a street so steep that it looked up-ended. At one side of it were steps, and at the top of the steps was a pretty little place with a balcony that promised a good view.

The place was clean and pleasant; we settled ourselves in a sunny corner of the balcony, and the proprietor brought us tea and ices and some unfamiliar-looking little cakes. We ate and drank and talked, for the most part, of the three happy days we had spent on board the *Juan Cortez*; the unhappy present receded. From life on board, we passed to comments on the people who were passing in the street below us. We felt warm and relaxed.

It was at that moment that I saw Senhor

70

Cunha.

I wouldn't have seen him if I had not been watching with some interest a dark, smartly dressed man who had limped down the steps to the street below. There had been a strong suggestion of haste and purpose in his descent, but when he reached the street, he paused, looked to right and left and then stood waiting for something, or somebody. He took a cigarette from his case and lit it—and the next moment had flung it down and taken a step in the direction in which he had been staring. Whatever, whoever he had been waiting for had arrived.

Following the direction of the lame man's glance, I saw that a large black car had stopped. Out of it stepped Luis Cunha.

I looked at Lindy and Rex. They had both seen him and they were both staring down in surprise. For a few moments none of us spoke; we were watching Senhor Cunha. He had walked up to the lame man and exchanged a brief greeting; the next instant they had both turned and Luis Cunha was following the lame man up the steps. Both had an air of haste and—I thought—secrecy.

They had reached the top of the steps before any of us moved; then Lindy leaned forward impulsively and called over the balcony.

'Mr Cunha!'

I could have sworn that he heard. I don't see how he could have helped hearing; Lindy's voice was high and clear, there were not many people about, and not much noise of traffic. But the lame man had already passed under the balcony; I could not see him, and when Lindy called, Senhor Cunha was just going out of view. I was nearest to the railing and therefore had the last glimpse of him before he went out of sight, and I was certain that he hesitated for an instant at the sound of his name. Then he had gone, and as the café was on a corner, we could not hope to see him again unless we went through the building to the front entrance.

I hesitated, but Lindy was on her feet.

'He didn't hear me. He may have news; let's follow him,' she said urgently. 'Come on, Rex. Come on, Aunt Kate.'

'But—'

'He may have heard something!' Lindy broke into my objections. 'Let's ask him—quickly! Quick, Rex, before he goes too far! He looked . . . I'm certain he looked as though he'd heard some news. Aunt Kate—come on!'

I was fumbling in my purse, trying to identify the unfamiliar money.

'You and Rex go ahead—hurry!' I said. 'I'll catch you up. Go on.'

They were gone, brushing past chairs and tables in their hasty progress through the café. I hurried after them, some paper money and some small change in my hand. The proprietor smiled at me in a friendly manner, but when I tried to make him understand that I was in a

72

hurry to pay the bill and leave, I found that his thinking processes, like Henry's, were deliberate. He went first to our table to count how many cakes we had eaten, and then got out pencil and paper to calculate what the total cost of them would be. By the time I had given him some money and he had laboriously worked out how much change he should give me, Rex was far down the street and Lindy nowhere to be seen.

I stood outside the café, hesitating; there was a narrow street to the left and an even narrower one to the right; before I could decide which way I should go, I saw to my amazement, backing cautiously from a doorway near the street on the left, the broad rear quarters of Senhor Cunha.

Without realizing that I had moved, I found that I had stepped back two paces and was standing screened by the jutting window of the café. I could see without being seen—and what I saw filled me with astonishment and alarm. Senhor Cunha came out of the doorway, and at a sign from him, the lame man followed; the two looked to right and left and I knew with certainty that they were waiting to see if any of us were in view. Then, with a burst of speed incredible both in the lame man and the unwieldy Cunha, they had gone across to the other side of the street and had turned into the one on the left.

A hand closed on my arm; with a startled

jerk, I turned. Lindy was standing beside me. Her face was white, but she looked calm and resolute.

'Come on,' she said.

'C—come on where?' I asked.

'We're going to follow them,' she said. 'But they mustn't see us. You saw, didn't you? They were dodging us.'

I opened my mouth to protest, or to argue, but Lindy had already left the shelter of the window and was drawing me after her. With all the haste, all the caution shown by the two men, we began to follow them.

We acted like experienced shadowers. We sheltered in doorways, peering out; as soon as Senhor Cunha had looked over his shoulder and assured himself that we were nowhere in sight, we came out and hurried on for some distance and then sheltered again. I couldn't have told why we were doing it; there had not been time to go into reasons, but I knew that Lindy, like myself, was convinced that Senhor Cunha's appearance was connected with Mr Barron's disappearance.

Before we had gone the length of the street, Senhor Cunha and his companion vanished. When I say vanished, I mean just that; one moment they were there, the next they were nowhere to be seen.

We walked forward cautiously until we reached the vanishing point, and we saw that the building in front of which we stood, and which had looked like one building, was in reality two; they were separated by an alley scarcely wide enough to accommodate two people walking abreast, especially if one of them happened to be Cunha, but it was along this alley that the two men had gone.

We walked into it and began at once to feel signs of claustrophobia. The buildings on either side were very high, shutting out almost all light; there were no doors to right or left; there was only the black alley, with the shaft of light at its end.

We went forward; I didn't know what we were going to find, and I was beginning to feel the beginnings of fear. I was also thinking more clearly, and I realized that if Cunha had any reason for wishing to remain unobserved, it was childish of us to expect him to account for his action. Moreover, time was passing and in less than an hour I must be on the ship; even if Luis Cunha could tell us anything that shed light on the mystery of Mr Barron's disappearance, I could do nothing but leave Lindy to pass the details on to Rex.

The thought of being late and missing the ship made my heart beat faster, but I told myself that having come so far down this dark alley, we might as well see what there was at the end of it.

There was a piece of waste ground at the end of it. It was not a large area, but it was foul and littered and smelt abominably and so strongly that after one breath I wanted to turn and go back to cleaner air.

But we had seen something: a small shack opposite to the end of the alley—and the shack was occupied. A thread of smoke trailed upward from a hole in the roof; some scrawny chickens pecked at the dust, a ragged infant played in the half-open doorway.

I found, to my horror, that I was trembling. Not fear, but exhaustion was making my limbs feel as though they belonged to somebody else. Desperately anxious that Lindy should not notice, I fumbled in my bag and brought out a handkerchief and pressed it tightly against my lips while I fought for self-control. To my relief, I felt myself becoming steadier, and with returning poise, I made up my mind what I was going to do: I was going to take Lindy away and advise her to tell Neil Harper and Alec Walsh what we had seen—and then she and Rex must say good-by to me and put me into a taxi, and I must go away.

And then the door of the shack opened fully, and Senhor Cunha faced us across the clearing. Behind him was the lame man. Behind the lame man was a third, not spruce and smart like the other two, but poorly clad.

The three stared at us for a moment, and then a woman darted forward from the shadows of the room and closed the door, leaving Senhor Cunha outside. As he walked towards us, I saw that his face looked gray.

'Have you any news?' asked Lindy, as he reached us.

'News?'

'Of my father?'

He recovered the poise he had lost so abruptly at the sight of us. He was shepherding us down the alley, talking as he went. No, there was, alas, no news of Mr Barron. The reason he had come to this place was that one of his servants was ill and had sent for him; he had come and he had seen him, and the man was to be moved to better quarters, the man and his wife and baby, and if only they had sent for him earlier, all this could have been done before and the man's recovery hastened.

I don't know what Lindy made of it. I was walking fast, and there was no time, no opportunity to study her reactions. For myself, I didn't believe a word of the story, except the bit about being sent for. But it was too late to surmise or to speculate; as we reached the café, Rex started forward to meet us, and I had looked at my watch and given a cry of dismay.

'Quick—a taxi!' I said.

'No. My car is here,' said Senhor Cunha. 'I will take you.'

I kissed Lindy, and Rex almost broke up my defenses by leaning forward and pecking me on the cheek.

'We'll come and see you off. There's lots of room in the car,' he said.

'No—no!' I cried. 'You and Lindy—you

77

must go home. And good luck, my darlings.'

'Your address!' cried Lindy. 'You forgot this morning.'

'Oh . . .' Once more I was groping in my bag. I brought out a pencil—and then something, a lack, a difference made me begin to search, at first without undue worry and then with mounting panic through the jumble of things in the handbag.

'I've got paper if you want it,' offered Rex.

'Not paper—no. No,' I mumbled, horror—stricken. 'It's not that.'

'What is it?' asked Lindy anxiously.

'It's . . .' I ended the hopeless search and stared at them. 'My passport. It's not here. It's—it's gone!'

There was a blank pause. I saw anxiety in the eyes of Rex, hope in Lindy's; in Senhor Cunha's was nothing but stark unbelief. But another look at me must have convinced him that I couldn't be as good an actress as all that; I knew that I was as white as chalk, and my knees were trembling. Every thought but one had flown out of my head: my grandson. I was on my way to him, and I had lost my passport.

The next two hours were pure misery, and so rushed and confused that I remember them only dimly. We were all in Senhor Cunha's car, going through the streets at a pace that sent me to my prayers. We skirted trams, dodged around buses and missed pedestrians by miracles. I was flung now against Lindy, now

78

against the cushioned Cunha. Then we were roaring up the street and into the drive and had stopped with a neck-breaking jerk at the door of the *Casa Roma*. We hurried inside and searched everywhere. No passport.

It might be in the restaurant. It might be in the café. Senhor Cunha undertook to look in both places and went quickly back to the car; we heard it roar away. Lindy came over to me and took my hand.

'Don't worry,' she said. 'He'll find it; it's sure to be in one place or the other.'

I said nothing. I was certain that it would be in neither one place nor the other. It had been in my bag when I went downstairs after washing in Lindy's bathroom. It had not—I knew now—been in the bag when I had been driving to the restaurant. With the clarity that comes sometimes in moments of desperation, I remembered looking into my bag as I had sat in the car beside Mr Searle. The passport had not been in the bag then; I had not noticed it at the time because I had not been thinking about passports, but I could see, now, the flap into which the passport fitted. I knew, now, that it had been empty then.

Someone had taken it out of my bag.

'Don't worry,' said Lindy again. 'Mr Cunha'll find it.'

But the time went by, and Senhor Cunha didn't return. A maid appeared, and then another; I saw a houseboy and realized that the servants had returned; Lindy went to the kitchen to speak to them. Rex went on searching for the passport; I searched for it, too, but I no longer hoped to find it. My mind was too confused to do more than record the certainty that it had been taken from my bag; when, or by whom, or why, didn't at this moment seem to matter. I clung to a slender thread of hope: that I might be wrong, that Senhor Cunha would appear, holding up the document I had never really cherished until now.

The sun went down, and almost at once it was dusk and then dark. Lindy and Rex were quiet; I stood at the window of the drawing room, looking out until there was nothing more to be seen.

I heard Lindy's voice beside me.

'Won't you come upstairs and rest just for a few moments, until Mr Cunha comes? You look awfully tired.'

I didn't want to rest, but I went upstairs. Lindy gave me fresh towels and left me in the bathroom, and I peered hopelessly about the fittings to see if the passport could by a remote chance have fallen out of my bag. But it was nowhere to be seen—and suddenly I knew that even if I found it now, it would be too late.

I walked out into the passage and wandered to a door on the opposite side; I wanted to find a room which had an outlook over the estuary. I wanted to see the water, and the docks—and the ships.

I opened the door. It was very dark, and I fumbled for a light, switched it on and then walked across the room and out onto a balcony. The view was beautiful: thousands of twinkling lights shone up at me from the city below, but I didn't really see them. I was staring at some lights on the water, and I knew that they were moving. They were moving away from the dock into the middle of the estuary. I watched them with a feeling of numbness, for I knew that they were the lights of the *Juan Cortez*. The ship had sailed—and I was left behind.

I turned and went back into the room, trying not to think. I stood there telling myself that people lost passports, missed buses and trains and ships and planes every day of the week. There was nothing to worry about; it would be all right.

I walked slowly to the door. For the moment, I could think of Lindy and Rex and be glad that they would be glad. I would go downstairs and we would talk it over cheerfully, and in the morning I would go out and see about getting another passport. I had no idea how I would get another passage, for I had scarcely any money.

I reached up to switch off the light. I have a memory of myself standing there, arm upraised, rigid with horror. I didn't find the switch and I didn't turn to look for it. My eyes were on the door of the bathroom which, like Lindy's, was an adjoining one. The door had been half open when I came into the room. Now it was closed. And from below it, creeping slowly into the bedroom and towards the thick gray carpet, was a thin trickle of red.

I stared at it, unable to move. Then I looked away, and waves of nausea came and went, leaving me trembling. I conquered my panic and forced myself to look once more at the spreading stain. I must be sure.

And I was sure. I was looking at a pool of blood.

CHAPTER FOUR

Most of us, I suppose, looking back over our lives, come across a number of things we're ashamed of. I come across more than most.

But I'm proud of what I did at that moment, because what I did was, in my opinion, very brave. Heroic. Perhaps having my passport stolen had made me impervious to lesser anxieties; perhaps I did what I did out of curiosity. I shall never know. All I can record is that after staring at the blood, I came to a conclusion: someone was in there, and whoever it was, was alive; alive enough to have shut the door. Someone was alive—and bleeding.

I walked across to the bathroom door and opened it.

There was a man inside, and he was hurt. I knew exactly where and exactly how badly, for he had no clothes on. He was one of the largest men I ever saw, and he was stark naked.

He was kneeling weakly beside the bath; he had managed to get some water into it and to remove his mud-stained clothing; now he was doing his best to wash the dirt from his scraped and bruised skin. One side of his body was caked with mud and blood. His efforts had caused an ugly gash on one of his arms to bleed freely. But there seemed no sign of serious injury.

It was not a moment for squeamishness. I leaned across and picked up a sponge and began to clean him up; he looked at me and began to say something and thought better of it. I turned on both taps, jerked a large towel off the rail, put it around him and with one foot hooked the bath stool nearer.

'Can you get up and sit on that?' I asked.

With my help, he got up. He sat, white-faced, as I washed as gently as possible the mud and dirt from him.

'Who're you?' he asked presently.

'Don't talk yet,' I said. 'I'm a friend of the children's—Lindy and Rex. Off the ship: You're their father and you've been in trouble, but I don't think—apart from losing a bit of blood—there's much wrong.'

I took what I needed from the big medicine chest on the wall. I worked in silence; most of the time his eyes were closed, but at last I saw that the color was returning to his face, and soon afterwards he opened his eyes and began to ask questions.

'Who's in the house?'

'Your children—and me. And the servants. They vanished for a time, but I think they've all come back.'

He thought this out. 'Police?' he said at last.

'Yes.'

'What happened today?'

'You were missing. Mr Walsh told the police, and they came here and questioned the servants. Everybody went out to look for you—except Mrs Rodrigues, but she came to the house at lunchtime; Mr Searle was here, too. The Cunhas gave us lunch—Lindy and Rex and myself—and ...' I hesitated, and then decided to leave for the moment the subject of my passport. 'I think it would be wise to send for Lindy and Rex as soon as you can; they've been through a bad day.'

He rose and went to the door of the bathroom and stood there for a moment to steady himself.

'There's a dressing gown in that cupboard,' he said.

I got it for him and he put it on. He spoke no word of thanks, but I was pleased with my handiwork; he looked clean and he was very

84

neatly bandaged; I had even brushed his hair. Looking at him now, I thought that his face was a little too rugged to be called handsome, but even in his present state he gave an impression of great firmness and strength and self-confidence. He had no thoughts to spare for me; he was engaged in his own concerns and for the moment I didn't matter and he didn't care whether he showed it or not.

'Send the children in,' he said, 'but don't tell anybody else I'm back—not yet.'

'What shall I tell Lindy and Rex? I can't just go down to them and tell them you're here. I'll have to explain that you're hurt.'

'Tell them what you like.' He was slumped in a huge chair, his legs stretched out in front of him, his head back against the cushion; he was pulling himself together. I noticed for the first time how gray his hair was; he must, I realized, be well over fifty, but his big body and strong face gave an impression of a man in his forties.

'If there's any food, I'd like some,' he said. 'And a drink. A drink first of all. A hell of a big drink. And soon.'

'I'll bring you one,' I said. I longed to know what had happened, but he had shown very plainly that he would not explain anything unless or until he wanted to. I guessed that he was a man who made a habit of using people; he was making use of me now, and for the moment I had no objection. But when he was stronger, I would tell him to get up and get his own hell of a big drink. But not now.

I walked out of the room—and straight into Neil Harper.

I don't know which of us, for the first few seconds, was the more taken aback. Neil, who had been walking down the corridor towards Lindy's room, stood frozen in his tracks, staring first at me and then over my head at the man seated in the room.

Mr Barron was the first to recover. He looked at Neil with a black frown and spoke in a voice thick with anger.

'What the hell—' he began.

Neil, with an effort, pulled himself together and spoke in a hurried and bewildered tone.

'I'm sorry, sir. I—' He looked at me. 'I went to the boat to see you off—you weren't there—and so I came to the house. Rex told me that your passport had been lost.' He looked at Mr Barron. 'He sent me up here to find Mrs Verney. Are you all right, sir?'

'Do I look all right?'

'You're alive,' said Neil simply.

'Did you think I was dead?'

'Yes,' said Neil.

'I see.' Mr Barron's voice was grim. 'How did you think I'd died?'

'I—' Neil stopped. 'I'm glad you're all right, sir,' he ended formally.

Mr Barron stared at him for a few moments.

'I was always of the opinion,' he said slowly, 'that you had a first-class brain. In the course

86

of the next few days, I might ask you to use it—on my behalf.'

'I'll be glad to, sir.'

He was gone, leaving Mr Barron looking after him thoughtfully. As he seemed to have nothing further to say, I followed Neil downstairs. He waited for me in the hall.

'Are you sending Lindy and Rex up to him?'

I nodded, and he smiled—a smile of deep relief.

'Thank God he's back,' he said fervently. 'When I left you and went up to the office and heard the news, I ...' He stopped. 'Go in and tell them,' he said.

He let himself out of the front door, and I went into the drawing room. Lindy and Rex turned, and I stood looking at them—but one look at my face was enough. Lindy was across the room and had seized my hands.

'You've got news—good news,' she said.

'Yes.'

'Father is ... is—' began Rex.

'Is upstairs,' I said. 'He's in his room. He's hurt, but not badly. He's waiting to see you both.'

Before I had finished speaking, they were halfway up the stairs. I left them for as long as I could, but I knew that Mr Barron would be a more affectionate father when he had his drink in his hand. I took one up to him.

I knocked and went in. He was still in the big chair; Lindy was sitting at his feet, her hands in his. Rex was looking on with a smile, and I wondered how long the smile would last, for it was clear to me, from the moment of entering the room, that Mr Barron had eyes for nobody but his lovely daughter. I wondered whether his son's room had been prepared with the same affectionate touches as Lindy's had been, and felt sure that it had not.

Mr Barron was telling them of his morning's adventures. I listened as I cleaned up some of the mess in the bathroom; I concluded that the servants were not to know in what state their master had returned. As I worked, I could hear Mr Barron's tale, and reflected that three or four days ago I had been in the pleasant position of being able to listen to people with a reasonable expectation of hearing them speak the truth. Today I had listened to so many lies that I was in a fair way to becoming a lie detector; I knew exactly when Mr Barron threw a grain of truth into his bushel of invention. Perhaps if I had been an affectionate child, newly reunited with this undeniably attractive father, I would have swallowed it whole. Lindy and Rex weren't fools and they knew how to listen intelligently, but Mr Barron was leaning back in his chair, glass in hand, talking in deep, brusque, assured tones, and he made his story sound very convincing.

I was on my way out of the room, leaving them together, when Mr Barron called me back.

'I haven't thanked you,' he said, 'but I'm grateful, all the same. I'm very glad you were here.' He looked at Lindy. 'You're the boss here now,' he told her. 'You'd better go downstairs and see about the arrangements for dinner.'

But Lindy did not move.

'I'll see to everything,' she said, 'but just at this moment I'd like to stay here.' She looked at her brother. 'Rex, would you go down and tell them that Father's here—and safe?'

Rex went out, but I don't think Mr Barron noticed that he had gone; he was looking at Lindy, this time with a new and measuring look. I waited for a moment and then asked somewhat abruptly if there was anything else I could do.

'Yes. Sit down, please, Aunt Kate,' Lindy answered.

I sat down on the edge of the bed. Lindy looked at her father and spoke gently.

'What you told us just now wasn't ... wasn't strictly accurate, was it?' He stared at her and she repeated the question more firmly. 'Was it, Father?'

'Didn't you believe any of it?' he asked after a pause.

'It sounded like the truth—in one or two places,' said Lindy. 'It's not the first time today we've listened to somebody performing impromptu.'

'Look, Lindy—' he began, but she put up a

89

hand and halted him.

'Wait, please,' she begged, and gave him an appealing smile. 'We're pretty mixed up as it is, and we'd like you to clear things up for us instead of making them more confused.'

'All right; the floor's yours. Tell me what you want me to clear up,' said her father.

'Did Mrs Verney tell you that she'd missed her boat?'

'She did.' He turned to me. 'Did you want to go, or did you want to stay and see this thing out?' he asked.

'Both,' I said. 'But the decision didn't rest with me at the end. My passport disappeared— and it didn't disappear all by itself. Somebody made it disappear.'

Lindy gave me a look, but it was not a look of surprise; she seemed about to say something, and then she had turned back to her father.

'Today has been ... dreadful,' she told him quietly. 'Not only because of you ... you didn't come, not because ...' She paused to steady her voice. 'People have been lying, and lying, and lying. People have been frightened, and they've been lying. Don't let's have any more lies, Daddy—please! Rex is a bit young to be told everything—but I'm not! Don't treat me like a ... as a child, please! If what happened today wasn't an ... an accident, say so right out clearly. Nothing's worse than feeling lost in lies—nothing! I'm not imagining any of this;

Aunt Kate—Mrs Verney will tell you it's all true. If we told you that her passport was stolen, would you think that I was exaggerating?'

He looked at us both and seemed to make up his mind.

'If I told you that I'd only just escaped being murdered this morning, would you think that I was exaggerating?'

Lindy stared at him, and I felt my heart sinking. Here at last was the truth, and it was ugly. Nobody spoke for some time, and then Mr Barron looked at his daughter.

'Well?' he asked.

'It was ... it was no surprise to you, was it?' said Lindy slowly.

Their glances seemed locked. They had forgotten I was in the room. I saw his brows meet in one of the black frowns that made his face grim and threatening, and he spoke to her in a low and dangerous voice.

'Who's been talking to you about me?'

Lindy appeared entirely unmoved by his anger.

'Nobody,' she told him. 'But since I came to Lisbon, nobody has said the one thing I've been listening for: a word of reassurance that nothing could possibly have happened to you—except by accident. Suspense is always bad, but today's suspense was worse than bad because I could feel that everybody was waiting to hear something terrible, something that was worse than an accident—even a fatal accident. They...'

Her voice faltered. Mr Barron, after a moment's deep thought, put out a hand and took one of hers; holding it closely, he began to speak in a steady and firm, but oddly gentle voice.

'Listen to me,' he said. 'If I'm going to tell you anything at all, I've first got to clear your mind of inaccuracies and get it working along the right lines. Understand this once and for all: I've been in this country a good many years, and I've never done anything I wasn't invited to do. And for the past few years, I haven't even responded to invitations. So if you're imagining that outraged husbands had wanted to injure me, I can only tell you that they could or would have done it long before this. Portuguese husbands, or brothers, or fathers, know their women pretty well; they know exactly how much is me, and how much is—the woman. The thing that happened to me this morning is absolutely unrelated to any of my actions in the past. Those things ... they happened a long time ago, and they don't explain what happened this morning. What happened this morning ...' He paused and his face darkened. 'It's new. It's recent. I ... I don't understand it.'

There was a long silence. At last he looked at me.

'Do you believe me?' he asked.

92

I hesitated. I thought of Sylvana Cunha in his study, searching among his papers. I remembered Neil Harper's words on the ship.

'I believe you,' said Lindy.

He looked at her.

'I'm glad. You won't be much use to me in this matter if you're going to let your mind roam over things that are past and done with. If you could believe that this is a new threat, then ... I can talk to you. And I want to talk to you. You're an incredibly lovely girl, but you're something else, too: you're a cool young woman and you look as though you could keep your mouth shut, and so I can tell you things I can't tell other people. Especially the people in the firm. Young Harper dislikes me—'

'That's nonsense—but go on,' put in Lindy.

'Searle's riddled with jealousy and suspicion and hates us all. Cunha's nursing a grudge. His wife is unreliable and Mrs Rodrigues is a liar. You can leave out Alec Walsh. I can talk to Alec, but he's much more than a business associate. He's a friend, and an old one, and he'd go through hell for me. In fact, he has; he saved my life. It's an old story and a war story and at the moment it's irrelevant, but you can take it from me that Alec is all right. And now—' he leaned back—'we can really talk.' He turned to me. 'Why was your passport stolen, and where, and when?'

'I had it before lunch,' I told him, 'and I didn't have it after lunch. The only people I've seen here have been the people in your firm, and even if it sounds fantastic, I'd be inclined to think that one of them must have taken it out of my bag—except for the fact that I got the impression from everybody that, on the whole, they'd rather have me out of the way. Stealing my passport would be a way of keeping me here—and nobody except Lindy and Rex appears to want me here. I've gathered a general impression that this is no time for a stranger to be around. So why should my passport disappear?'

Mr Barron spoke slowly.

'It could disappear,' he pointed out, 'because somebody else wanted to use it.'

I said nothing, but my mind didn't dwell long on this theory. Mr Barron hadn't seen my passport photograph, and I saw no point in telling him that anybody wishing to use it as their own would be in for a humiliating time. Half moron, half monster; I wished them luck.

'For the moment,' I said, 'the passport doesn't matter. What happened to you?'

We had to wait some time before he told us; he was staring straight ahead expressionlessly, and I knew that he was living it all over again.

'I ride every morning,' he said slowly at last. 'I stable my horses here, but the groom takes the horse or horses out early, and I drive out and meet them and do my riding on a piece of ground I own a few miles out of Lisbon. There's a short cut from the road to the open

94

ground. It's up a hill and along a narrow and dangerous ledge. There's only room for one horse with a man aboard, and nobody uses the path except myself, because it's considered a crazy risk. I take it because I've complete confidence in my horses—and complete control over them. There's no danger of crumbling—it's rocky. At the far end of the ridge, the path widens a bit, and the horse sees he's over the worst part and getting onto more open ground, and he likes to speed up a bit, and as a rule I let him. This morning—'

He stopped, and his face set slowly into hard, dangerous lines. We waited, but it was some time before he went on. At last Lindy prompted him.

'This morning?'

'This morning, I let him out. Twenty seconds later, he was over the edge. He died at once, thank God. The drop is ... lethal.'

'And ... and you?' she breathed.

'I went over, too, and I should have gone to the bottom, as he did. But I'm a hard man to kill—and today, nature was on my side. I went down a good way, and then I got hung up on the branch of a tree. I saw the horse go down. Have you ever heard a horse scream?'

'No.'

'You're very fortunate. I hung there for some time because I wasn't in any state to try to unhitch myself; then I felt a bit steadier, and I managed to get off the branch and—

eventually—to crawl up the side of the hill. I wanted to get up there again—for many reasons. The main one was to make certain that I'd seen ... what I'd seen. And when I'd crawled up at last, it was there. Wire.'

He paused, but we could only stare at him.

'Was it—' began Lindy.

'It had been stretched across the path—short, taut and effective. Around a rock on one side, around a tree on the other. A clumsy way to kill a horse and a man, but—as I said—effective. There was one chance in a hundred that I'd come out of it alive. But before I crawled up again—and as I told you, it took some time—the wire had been cut and the ends had been pushed into the thick undergrowth on either side of the path. Only somebody who knew what he was looking for, and who knew where to look, could have found them.'

There was another silence. Through it I heard, in my imagination, the scream of a horse.

'How did you get home?' asked Lindy at last.

'I waited to see if the groom came to see what had happened. But when I'd waited for some time, I understood that if I had heard the horse, so had he. He must have come looking—and he must have seen the wire. If he had, it wouldn't take him long to understand what had happened and to write me off as dead. But like the other servants, he wouldn't feel there was anything he'd like to tell the police, and so

96

he'd fade out of the picture until the time for answering questions—awkward questions—had passed.'

'Could he have had anything to … to do with it?' asked Lindy.

'No.' Mr Barron's voice held complete certainty. 'No. I don't know how he feels about me, but I know how he feels about the horses. He couldn't hurt one of them.'

'Then how did you—'

'Get here? I managed to get back to my car, and I drove it out of the way of searchers. When it was dark, I drove home. I left the car out in the road and came in by way of the garden. I climbed up onto the balcony and got in that way. I didn't want Lindy to see me as I was.'

'Or Rex,' I said.

'Or Rex. And now I want to get on the phone to Alec and ask him to get around here as soon as possible. And I want the police informed of my safe return, and I don't want them around any more.'

'But—' began Lindy.

'But what? But why not let them investigate this? I'll do my own investigating. I'm not going to have a posse of policemen nosing about the house just when you've got here.'

'And Rex,' I said.

'And Rex. I'll do my own investigating. Not that there'll be much need to investigate; if somebody wants me out of the way as badly as

97

this, they'll have another shot at it. They won't stop at one try. Only—next time—I'll see it coming. I hope.'

'But you can't go on as though ... as though nothing had happened!' said Lindy.

'Which is better?' he asked. 'To bring in the police and have them in and out of the house, questioning, shadowing, reminding us, worrying us all—or to keep the thing to ourselves, to say as little as possible to everybody and to say nothing at all to Rex; to stick to the story I told you just now?' He smiled at Lindy. 'I don't want you worrying.'

'Or Rex,' I said.

'I've been thinking about this thing all day,' he said, 'and I've got it fairly straight, and that's what I think is best. I'll get Alec here and ask him what he makes of it all.'

He leaned forward and stretched out a hand, and Lindy pushed the telephone forward until he could reach it. He picked up the receiver and looked at me.

'Will you see that a message gets through to the Cunhas and to Searle and Athena? Say I'm back, nothing more. Same story as I dished out just now. They won't believe it, but that's not important. The same goes for the servants. And if you could make them hurry up with some food, I'd be grateful. And I'd like another drink.'

I went out. As I closed the door behind me, I heard Mr Barron's voice and I felt a wave of relief as I remembered Alec Walsh's calmness and strength and reliability. Once he got here, things would assume a more normal, a more natural appearance. I went down the corridor feeling considerably cheered.

Then I stopped with the depressing realization that I had nowhere to go. I was in the house not as a guest, not even as a visitor, but as a stranger whose carelessness had left her on the hands of anybody who would help her out of her predicament.

There was no time to pursue this thought. The door of Mr Barron's room had opened; Lindy came out and called to me. She led me into a room farther down the corridor; I saw that it was a large, pleasant bedroom and that it had been prepared for my use. A door with glass panels, leading onto the balcony, stood open; the bed was turned down, flowers stood in vases here and there. I saw an adjoining bathroom with pale blue fittings and a pile of fluffy blue towels.

'Yours,' said Lindy, and studied me for a moment. 'You look tired. You ought to have your dinner in bed.'

'I won't do that,' I said, 'but I'd like to fall into bed immediately afterwards.'

'Then you shall,' said Lindy. She came forward and gave me a fervent hug. 'Oh, I'm so happy,' she breathed. 'Everything's all right again.'

Rex appeared in the doorway and grinned.

'Not for Aunt Kate,' he pointed out. 'She hasn't got any luggage.'

'I'll lend you things for the night,' Lindy told me, 'and in the morning we'll go shopping. You're not to worry about anything. It's our fault that you missed the boat, and Daddy's going to see to everything.'

I thought Mr Barron would have enough on his mind without adding my problems to his own. I didn't say so, however; I asked Rex to telephone the Cunhas and Mrs Rodrigues and Mr Searle to tell them of his father's safe return, and arranged to meet Lindy downstairs as soon as I was ready for dinner.

And then I was alone, with leisure to sort out my impressions. I was stranded without a passport in the house of a man who had that morning narrowly escaped being murdered. I was stranded with nothing but the clothes I stood up in, with scarcely any money and without any idea how I could continue my journey. I tried to guess what steps were taken by the authorities when a passenger was left behind in a foreign port; would they notify the police? Would they send word to London, and would Henry get to hear of it?

Henry ... solid, stolid Henry.

He couldn't, just then, have seemed farther away if he'd been living on another planet. This wasn't Henry's world. This was a world in which men walked in danger of violent death, in which people stole and lied.

I was walking to and fro without knowing what I was doing—but my pacing had brought me to the balcony, and when I looked out into the night, I forgot all my troubles and all Mr Barron's troubles, too. I stood staring at the entrancing sight before me.

I was looking at the myriad lights of the city. I had seen them before, when I had stood on Mr Barron's balcony, which was next to this one. But I had noticed little, then, but the lights of the *Juan Cortez* moving steadily away, leaving me behind. Now I could take in more details. I saw that below the balcony was a large garden, at the end of which was a road; like the road which ran in front of the house, it was quiet and rather dark and unfrequented. I could see the outlines of trees, some of them very close to the house; I could put out my hand and touch palm trees. At my feet, plants grew and spread over the railing of the balcony; there were flowers growing in pots and in boxes. Far away, I saw a faint gleam of moonlight on the waters of the Tagus. It was beautiful and soothing and restful. It had nothing to do with violence and mystery.

I turned and went into the bedroom, feeling considerably calmer. I would send a cable to Sue and her husband and tell them that I would take the next available boat.

I had a bath in water that seemed to have a faintly blue tinge; I wondered whether it would have a bleaching effect. I dressed once more in the suit which by now I deeply loathed. I saw that Lindy's absurd little pajamas had been laid on my bed.

I went downstairs and received at once proof that the staff had indeed reappeared; no sooner had I entered the drawing room than a white-coated man appeared and asked me what I would drink. He brought me sherry, placed cigarettes, almonds and olives at my elbow and withdrew, and I was left to settle myself against the sofa cushions and wonder how I should like this sort of attention every night at home, instead of eating olives straight from the bottle and drinking my sherry as I whipped myself up an omelette for my dinner. In this quietly luxurious room, it was impossible to believe that horror lurked beneath the smooth surface of life. I might pretend that all was normal, all as it should be—and then I seemed to see a narrow path along the shoulder of a cliff, and a horse and a man falling, falling...

The door opened. I looked up expecting to see Lindy or Rex, but it was Alec Walsh who came in, and his handsome face was pale. He stood for some moments frowning down at me, but I knew that he wasn't seeing me. He came to himself with a start and walked over to the table and poured himself out a drink.

'Will you do something for me?' he asked.

'If I can.'

'Will you, or you and Lindy between you, try to persuade Barron to use some sense and call in the police?'

I stared at him.

'But he said—' I began.

'He's called them off. He rang them up and told them that he was back, and safe, that he had no further need of them. He told them that his horse went over and that he managed to get himself up the hill again. He said nothing to them about ... anything else.'

'I've got no influence with him.'

'You can tell him to think of Lindy and Rex. He might listen to you, but I can't move him.'

'But why won't he tell them what happened and ask them to ... to investigate it quietly, to—'

'It's just the way he's made.' He walked over, drink in hand, and stood looking down at me. 'There's a quotation somewhere about an Englishman; I don't remember exactly how it goes, but it's something about "being flattered, a lamb; threatened, a lion." Well, that's Bill Barron. At the moment, he can't see anything beyond the fact that somebody tried to kill him. If he were a reasonable man, that would frighten him. As it is, he's fighting mad. He wants to get his hands around the throat of whoever it was—'

'That would be all very well if he only had himself to think about,' I broke in. 'But how does he think that Lindy and Rex can stay here if there are going to be more attempts of this kind?'

103

'I've pointed that out to him. Results negative. I think he might listen to you.' He frowned. 'This is a hell of a thing for you to be mixed up in,' he said.

'I don't suppose I'll be mixed up in it long. I hate to speak of my own affairs,' I said, 'but there are certain—'

'Do forgive me. I ought to have referred to that as soon as I came in. Bill asked me to make it clear that you're not to worry about anything. The office will fix your passport and your passage and any purchases you may have to make. The only reason you're stranded in Lisbon is because Lindy and Rex needed you. We're very grateful to you and we won't have you bothering about anything. There's every chance of our being able to arrange a passage for you in three or four days; if you'll write out a cable for your daughter, I'll see that it's sent off—and any others that you need to send.'

'No others,' I said. Certainly Henry wasn't going to hear of this. 'Mr Walsh—'

I had been about to ask his views on the disappearance of my passport, but the door had opened to admit Lindy, and she had something of her own to say to him.

'Mr Walsh,' she began, without preamble, 'Mrs Verney and I saw something in the study this morning that we both thought ... odd. I haven't mentioned it to my father yet, because there hasn't been any opportunity—but unless you feel he should know about it, I think I'd rather not tell him, at any rate not yet.'

'Why not?' asked Alec.

'Because I think he's got enough on his mind, and if you can tell us whether you feel it's too important to be kept from him—'

'What is it?' he asked.

'Senhora Cunha was in the study, looking through Daddy's papers. There's probably no reason why she shouldn't have been, if her husband asked her to, but . . . she didn't look as though she wanted to be found there. She went out by the long window, and we saw her purely by accident, but—'

'When was this?' asked Alec.

'This morning, just before lunch. She and her husband drove away after having arranged to meet us for lunch. Mr Searle went away, too, in his own car. But when Senhora Cunha was in the study, there was no sign of their big car; there was a car waiting in the drive, but it was . . . it was Mr Searle's.'

The room seemed very quiet when she stopped speaking. It was some time before Alec's voice was heard.

'Sylvana Cunha,' he said slowly, 'isn't the first woman who has written an indiscreet letter to your father, and then regretted it. But—' he gave her a smile that had something warm and fatherly in it—'please don't allow yourself to get a wrong idea of him. Your father is . . . all right. Perhaps he has too good a time; perhaps he doesn't select his friends too carefully; perhaps he takes them too much on trust.'

The smile had faded; he looked almost somber. Lindy put out a hand and touched his for an instant.

'You know him better than anybody else,' she said quietly.

'I've known him for over twenty years. You must believe me,' said Alec, 'when I tell you that there's not a better man anywhere. But he's a man who has always done things in his own way, without worrying too much how it would affect other people. When it comes to women, he isn't likely to take advice, but I can assure you that as far as I know, he has never looked twice at Sylvana. The Cunhas—' his voice grew perceptibly cooler—'aren't easy to understand. I don't pretend to know how their minds work.'

I thought of what Athena had told me, and put a question.

'Could there have been a ... a threatening letter on Mr Barron's desk? If Senhora Cunha had—'

'Do you know,' asked Alec, 'whether she found what she was looking for?'

'No,' said Lindy.

'That's a pity.'

'Should we tell my father?'

'At the moment, no; if you'll leave it to me, I'll bring it up with Cunha at an opportune moment. Until then, I should say nothing. As you said just now, your father's got enough on his mind.'

He was about to say more, but at that moment the door opened and Rex came in with Robert Searle. I learned that he was staying to dinner, and so was Alec Walsh, and I saw that my hopes of eating punctually and going to bed immediately dinner was over were vain ones. Nobody appeared to feel that there was any hurry to eat. Alec Walsh led Rex to the table and introduced him to a nonalcoholic drink called Totem, and the two stood there chatting with the timeless air that men all over the world seem to assume when someone has gone to the trouble of cooking them a good meal and is waiting to set it before them.

Mr Searle stood talking to Lindy; when she came over to join me, he went upstairs to see Mr Barron; no sooner had he come down again, when the door opened once more and Athena Rodrigues came in with the Cunhas. I resigned myself to an evening of semi-starvation.

Mr Walsh brought me a sherry. It was my third, and I didn't want it. I left it untasted and sat marveling at the amenities of life in Lisbon, where servants waited without impatience to serve meals when their masters would be ready for them. In England, Henry's married couple would by now have made it clear that dinner was ready and that if Henry and his wife weren't, good-by.

Senhor Cunha came over and lowered himself onto the sofa between Lindy and myself. His wife was talking to Alec Walsh; Alec's manner, I saw, had lost the warm, easy friendliness with which he had talked to Lindy and myself; he was far more formal, far more cool. To Cunha he had given no more than a nod, and he seemed oblivious to Athena's efforts to gain his attention.

But Senhor Cunha had no difficulty in gaining Lindy's and mine. He had addressed us with a casual air that made it appear to the others as though he were talking of trivial matters, but his voice was pitched low and his words could not be overheard.

'There is something I must say to you both,' he said. 'We met this afternoon; you saw me with a lame man and you hoped that I might have news of Mr Barron.'

'Yes,' said Lindy.

'I explained that I had no news.'

'We heard you explaining,' said Lindy, in a dry little voice.

He smiled. It was not a wide smile, but there was something about it that was oddly appealing; his eyes—magnificent brown eyes that were his only attractive feature—lit for a moment with a gleam of amusement, and in that instant I found myself wondering why my first impressions of him had been so unfavorable. Before I could pursue this reflection, he had put another question.

'Have you, either of you,' he asked, 'mentioned this meeting to anybody?'

'No,' I said.

'Not yet,' said Lindy.

'May I beg that you will not?'

We looked at him in astonishment.

'Isn't that rather absurd?' asked Lindy in her turn. 'Even if Mrs Verney and I said nothing, my brother—'

'Your brother,' he pointed out quietly, 'will perhaps speak of the incident, but I do not think that he attached any special significance to it, and so no harm will be done when he gives his version of the meeting. But if you give yours, Miss Barron, or if Mrs Verney gives hers, a great deal of harm will be done.'

Lindy gave him a long, searching look.

'I don't understand you,' she said bluntly at last.

'Let me explain. Your brother saw me—but he did not see where I went. He does not know … what you and Mrs Verney know. And it is what you and Mrs Verney know that, for the present, nobody else should know. I cannot do more than ask you to believe that it is very important to say nothing. I cannot even explain further. I can only hope that you will believe me when I tell you that for me to try to explain matters further to you at this stage would not only confuse you hopelessly, but would also complicate the situation and cause great trouble. Please believe this.'

109

Lindy opened her mouth to say something, but Senhor Cunha had glanced up and had seen his wife coming towards us, and was saying smoothly:

'and so you see, Miss Barron, Portugal has, after all, a stirring history.' He rose and took his wife's hand. 'We are going?'

'Yes,' she said. 'It is late.'

'I am ready,' he said. She went to make her farewells and for a moment he stood looking down at us. I don't know what he saw; what we saw was a short, fat, dark little Portuguese who had lied to us that afternoon and who might have the most sinister reasons for wanting us to remain silent.

'Well?' he asked.

I saw Lindy hesitate.

'All right,' she said at last, and I nodded.

Once more Senhor Cunha smiled. He bowed to us both.

'Thank you,' he said, and turned to Lindy. 'You have something, Miss Barron—both you and Mrs Verney—that is better than intelligence. You have sound instincts.'

He left us to digest this dubious compliment. I sat turning over the conversation in my mind, and was recalled disagreeably by the sound of Lindy's voice asking Athena if she would care to stay and dine. She accepted at once.

'Alec,' she asked, 'will you phone and tell them I won't be back to dinner?'

He went out. Rex went upstairs with Robert

Searle to see if Mr Barron wanted anything, and Lindy and I were left with Athena. She came to sit near us, and then turned to me and gave me a long, frank, far-from-admiring top-to-toe look.

'If I make remarks about your appearance, I hope you won't mind,' she said. 'I do it to every woman I meet if she interests me. But for heaven's sake, don't go and get offended. Did Sylvana offer to take you shopping tomorrow?'

'No.'

'She's a selfish little brute. If you'd been young and glamorous, she would have taken you around to all her pet shops and made them look after you but—she's not interested in women over forty. Except me, of course; she keeps her eye on me because she's afraid of me. I tell you what: I'll take you shopping tomorrow.'

'I was going to take Mrs Verney,' said Lindy. 'My father—'

'You can come, too,' said Athena coolly. 'But if Mrs Verney goes alone with you, she'll buy what she likes. If she goes with me, she'll buy what she should. You won't mind my saying, will you,' she asked me, 'that women like you make the blood go to my head?'

'Make the—'

'I get angry. I get mad. Why? Because I've got a theory that as women get older, they've got to wage perpetual war. Old age—let's face it—is damned ugly. There's not much that men can do to stave it off; they have to look ghastly and lump it, poor devils, but women can and should look attractive. Even ugly ones. So when I see a woman like you, who's got so much and who wastes it all, If I'm making you angry, just stop me.'

'You needn't stop. My daughter used to say the same thing, only in a more personal vein. In a way, it was a relief when she went to South America.'

'I think,' said Lindy, the angry pink showing in her cheeks, 'I think Mrs Verney looks very nice indeed.'

'She will do when I've finished with her,' said Athena, and turned to me. 'All you need, if you'll forgive me for saying so, is a bit of pulling in there—'

'Ouch!'

'—and there.'

'If you've got rolls of flesh, you've got them,' I said. 'If you cram them in one end—I've tried it—they bulge out the other. So what's the use? This way, I'm comfortable.'

'I can see you are. Tomorrow you'll be less comfortable, and the bulges will be bulging evenly. You'll spread the load, that's all. Of course you'll be hellishly uncomfortable, but what do you expect?'

'A woman is a dresser—or she isn't,' I said. 'If she isn't, she doesn't mind looking like ... like me.'

'Tomorrow,' said Athena, 'you're going to make the most of a golden opportunity and you're going to buy yourself some decent things. The firm's giving you an open check; nothing personal; just because we all had something to do with your missing the boat. We'll shop first and have lunch afterwards. I'll ring you up tomorrow and fix a time.'

'But—'

'It'll be a pleasure,' said Athena grimly. She looked up as Alec Walsh came in. 'Alec, darling, will you bring me a drink?'

'No. We're all hungry,' he said. 'I think it's time we dined.'

His tone was friendly but not warm. I saw Athena's hands tighten on the arm of her chair. I thought she was on the point of saying something, but at that moment Rex came in with Robert Searle.

'Dinner,' said Lindy, pulling me to my feet. 'I'm sorry we've kept you so late.'

When dinner was over, I said good night to the others and went upstairs. I was full of good food and good wine and I was going to have a good night's rest in a good bed.

But not yet. As I reached the top of the stairs, the door of Mr Barron's room opened and he looked out at me.

'Can you spare a moment?' he asked.

I went into his room and he closed the door. There was a marked hesitation before he offered me the chair; reluctantly, I told him that he had better have it, and went to sit on the bed.

'I spoke to Alec,' he said. 'Did he say anything to you?'

'Yes. He says you've got to call the police in.'

'Well, I won't. Not yet, anyway. Were there any fireworks downstairs?'

'Fireworks?'

'That's what I said.' He ran a hand through his hair. 'God only knows what's the matter with everybody. The whole crowd—Alec, Athena, Searle, the Cunhas—they all seem to be at one another's throats. I suppose you wouldn't believe me if I told you that a week ago, we were a humdrum firm with nothing out of the ordinary about any of us, and that we were all, on the surface at any rate, on friendly terms. Now ... I'm a potential murderee, young Searle's mixed up in some way with Sylvana, and Alec and Cunha are at loggerheads.'

'Have they quarreled?'

'They had a disagreement when they went across to London a few days ago. They went together, to interview a new fellow who's coming out to join the office here. He—'

'Charles Essex?'

'Yes. How did you—Oh, through young Harper, of course.'

'Yes. He mentioned him on the boat, and said that they were old friends.'

'Harper ... Yes, I'd forgotten you all came
114

over together. What did you think of him?'

'I liked him very much.'

'And Lindy?'

I hesitated.

'She thought, at first, that he was a little dull—or at any rate tongue-tied.'

'There's nothing the matter with his tongue—if he cares to use it. But mostly, he doesn't. Pity he accepts his father's view of me. The old judge never liked me.'

'Judge?' I thought of the stern, upright figure in the train. 'Yes, he looked like a judge.'

'You know him?'

'No. I saw him for a moment when he was seeing his son off at the station in London.'

'Reluctantly, I dare say; he'd like to see him out of the firm. But I wouldn't. After Alec, he's the best man we've got. He's got his father's brain, and that's why he got ahead of Searle.' He raised his arms above his head and gave a great sigh. 'Come to think of it, Essex seems to be the cause of this breakdown of friendly relations throughout the firm. I think Searle's going to chuck his hand in because Essex is coming in over his head. Sylvana's probably on Searle's side. Alec's angry with Cunha because they had a disagreement over the appointment of Essex—and Cunha won. Cunha's nursing a grievance because he wanted me to take his brother into the firm, instead of another Englishman—and I refused.' He moved restlessly. 'Well, to hell with the firm's rows;

I've got enough on my mind. From now on, I'm ceasing to be a man of habit. The only reason I came so close to a finish this morning was because somebody knew exactly what I was going to do, and when. If you're a man of fixed habits, you're easy to trap. After this, I'm not going to follow any set routine. Everything I do in the hours outside the office will be up to Lindy.'

'And Rex. And inside the office?'

'That'll be up to Alec. He's been bodyguard for me before; he'll do it again. But if you think—' his face hardened—'if you think I'm going to let some murdering swine get away with this, you're mistaken. But you needn't fear for Lindy; nothing'll happen to her.'

'Or Rex?'

He gave me a look of irritation.

'You keep playing that record,' he said. 'What's it all about?'

'You've got two children, not one. I saw what you did in Lindy's room, and it was nice of you. I didn't see whether you did the same for Rex or not.'

'I did not,' he said belligerently. 'So? A girl's a girl; you can pet her. A boy of that age is, or ought to be, a man. What did you expect— roses in his room?'

'He's your son, and he's every bit as nice a boy as Lindy is charming a girl. If you think I'm going to watch you sitting there and looking adoringly at Lindy and looking

116

straight through Rex because, as far as you're concerned, he just isn't there, you're due for a surprise. I think you're a—'

I paused.

'You think?' he prompted.

The half-sneer in his voice touched off the last of my self-control. I was tired—and on this subject, I had been bottled up too long. I stood up.

'I think,' I told him, 'that you're a selfish, self-indulgent man and, in my opinion, which nobody has asked, you're not equipped to understand what a privilege it is merely to have produced two nice young people like Lindy and Rex. I think you're prepared to take over where your wife left off, but you won't go on building. You'll destroy all the good principles she instilled into them and all the goodness and the charm and the ... the innocence, simply by being what you are. You've brought them out here for your own pleasure, without one thought of whether you can provide a good background—a *good* background—for them. I've brought up two children as nice as yours are, and I know that the job can't be done as you're planning to do it. At this moment, you're preparing to invite a murderer to come and have another go at you. You like danger. You'll enjoy every moment. And in between his attempts, you'll take Lindy out and show her to your friends and beam with pride—and you'll send Rex back to England in a month

117

knowing perfectly well that you haven't any time for him and that, as far as you're concerned, it wouldn't matter if he never came out here again. I don't like you, Mr Barron, or anything about you, and I wish with all my heart that I'd never got on that boat and met your children and got to care so much what happened to them. And I hope you'll get me another passage and let me get away from here as quickly as possible.'

I was at the door, and I was practically choking with rage and hate—but I had said a fraction of what I had wanted to say, and I was feeling better. I couldn't see his face; he hadn't bothered to turn his head, and for all I knew, he'd stopped listening. But I still felt better; the pressure was down a bit.

I opened the door and took a firm grip. I'm no doorbanger, but this one, I resolved, was going to come off its hinges. Then I heard his voice.

'Mrs Verney.'

Like a fool, I turned. He was standing looking at me, and he was grinning, and the grin gave his face an unexpectedly boyish look.

'Did anybody,' he asked, 'ever try to murder you?'

It didn't come quite off its hinges. But almost.

CHAPTER FIVE

I went to bed that night to dream not of Mr Barron and his two children, nor of the members of his firm; I was on a swaying ship, in an almost empty dining saloon, and Neil Harper and I were sitting alone at a table, eating olives and almonds. He was illustrating on the tablecloth the defense of the Peninsular; the knives made the line of fortifications, and Wellington was the pepper pot.

It was a restless sleep. In the morning, a maid brought me my tea; on the tray was a large envelope with a Lisbon postmark which I glanced at, but did not trouble to open; I knew what it contained. I leaned against the pillows thinking of the events of the day before; I had hoped that this morning I might have been able to find reasons for some of the things which had baffled me in yesterday's confusion, but even after drinking three cups of tea to stimulate my brain, I could make no sense of anything that had occurred. I had a gloomy feeling that literature had let me down. All that Sherlock Holmes—for nothing.

Opening the envelope and slipping my passport into my bag, however, I realized that on one point I had reached a very definite conclusion: the fact that the only time my handbag had been out of my sight on the day before was the moment when I went to the front door to admit Alec Walsh. I had left the bag in the drawing room—with Athena.

I was dressed when Lindy knocked at the door. She came in and kissed me.

'Did you sleep well?' she asked.

'Yes, thank you. How is your father this morning?'

'He's fine—he's going to the office after breakfast. There's a telephone call for you,' she said. 'It came through in Daddy's room, next door.'

'Who is it?'

'I don't know. Daddy didn't say.'

Lindy left me at the door of her father's room, and went downstairs. The door was open, and I saw that Mr Barron was fully dressed. With no clothes on, he had looked impressive; in a dressing gown he had been imposing, but in a suit he seemed to fill the room. He nodded; I said good morning and took up the receiver to speak to what I fully expected to be Athena, ringing to tell me when and where we were to meet.

It wasn't Athena, however.

'Oh—Neil!' I said in surprise.

Mr Barron had walked out onto the balcony. At the sound of the words, he turned and walked slowly back; he came up to the table and stood looking down at me with a puzzled frown on his face. I scarcely noticed; I was listening with a pleasure that surprised me to the dry, formal young voice on the phone.

'Will you and Lindy have lunch with me today?'

'Lunch?' I thought of Athena and the shopping expedition. 'No, we can't do lunch, I'm afraid. We're being taken out by a glamorous woman who's going to smarten me up.'

'Please stay as you are,' said Neil. 'Will you both come to dinner?'

'I'd love that, thank you. I'm not sure about Lindy.'

'Call for you—one or both—at seven-thirty,' he said, and rang off. I put down the receiver and Mr Barron spoke.

'That Harper?' he asked.

'Yes.'

'You got to know him pretty well on the boat, I gather.'

'Where did you gather it from?'

'From watching Lindy's face whenever his name's mentioned. Think she's interested in him?'

'Why don't you ask her?' I asked.

'Where are you meeting him?'

'He's calling for us here.'

'Good. I'll see him then,' he said. 'I'd like a word with him. Can't say what I want to say at the office.'

I felt the familiar warning stirring the hairs at the top of my head.

'You won't have much time for talking,' I

said. 'We'll be on our way out.'

'I suppose I can talk to a fellow in my own house.'

'You can't keep us waiting while you whisk our escort off to your study for a nice chat.'

He came over and leaned on the table again, looking down as he had done before, but this time he was grinning like an impertinent schoolboy.

'Hasn't your doctor ever told you,' he asked, 'that you mustn't get overexcited?'

'I'm not overexcited; I'm just angry, that's all. You've got an overriding manner that I don't care for. You're wasted here, you know; you ought to have been one of those feudal barons, lording it over the serfs.'

I got up and we looked at one another.

'If you think I'm going to talk to him about keeping away from my daughter,' he said, 'you're wrong. I want to talk to him about the new fellow who's coming out to the firm. And if you're going out with Athena, you might tell her that Harper's come to life.'

'To life?'

'Yes. Athena always said that as far as women were concerned, he was stone dead. But now observe: after three days on board, he's ringing up and taking Lindy out to dinner. And cutting the ground from under my feet by taking you, too.' He gave a slow, appreciative smile. 'He's got his father's brain. Did you know that his father used to be the most famous judge in England?'

'I haven't the talent for screwing information out of strangers.'

For the first time, I heard him laugh. His amusement turned him from a rather surly, brooding man into the pleasant-faced and attractive father of two attractive children.

'What,' he asked, as I went to the door, 'is Athena going to do to you?'

'Smarten me up. I'm going to look like her.'

'Do you want to look like her?'

'Not in the least, but it'll be interesting to see how far short of the target I fall.'

'According to my children, you'll do very well as you are,' he said.

'According to my children, too. Perhaps more women would look as sleek and smooth and groomed as Athena if they had more time to work at it. But I use up a lot of time making a living.'

His eyebrows went up.

'You work?'

'On and off. Before the children married, I worked all the time. Now I work until I save a little money, and then I travel till it runs out. At the moment I'm traveling.'

'What do you work at?'

'When my husband died, I went into a shop and stayed there learning one or two things; then I took a room near Regent Street and began to sell babies' clothes. Nothing useful; just frothy little bits of muslin, and smocked rompers, and ribbon-and-lace confections. I did well and ended up in a little shop of my own. No sensational success, but a steady turnover and a nice profit when I sold it. Now I help them intermittently—between travels.'

'Do you live alone now?'

'Yes. The bills for the morning's expedition, I understand, are on the firm?'

'To the limit. It's the least we can do. See you at breakfast.'

We must have looked very domesticated, the four of us: Father off to the office, Mother going on a shopping spree, children going out to explore the town. That was the superficial view, however; it was Lindy who sat at the head of the table and poured coffee; the courteous attention Rex paid me never came from any son—and nothing was less like father-off-to-work than Mr Barron, with his unopened letters and newspapers and his obvious delight in having the company of his children at breakfast.

Shopping with Athena turned out to be—for me—an extremely successful morning. After the first few moments in the first shop, when I had blanched at the price tags, I remembered that for almost the first time in my life I could buy without the usual aftermath of regret or remorse or panic—and after that it was all pure pleasure. A woman cursed all my life with financial qualms, on that morning I had none; I reminded myself that the firm of Barron and

124

Walsh had been the means of my losing my ship and my passport and an early meeting with Sue; I did not feel that they owed me the gratitude they had expressed, but I felt that they owed me an apology.

They made a handsome one. While Athena and Lindy disagreed hotly over color and style and type, I bought a day dress, an evening dress, two pairs of shoes and some underwear, and some pajamas of a more sensible kind than Lindy's. And whether it was the Lisbon air or the exhilarating feeling of watching somebody else signing the checks, the end of the morning found me as fresh as I had been at the beginning. Instead of feeling too exhausted, as I did at home after some hard shopping, to do more than crawl on a bus and go home to coffee and a salad, this morning I was ready to do it all over again. So was Lindy. The one who was flat out was Athena.

'Never again,' she moaned, as we took our seats at a table for lunch. 'Never again, so help me! Never!'

'You didn't expect to repair the neglect of years in a couple of hours, did you?' I asked her. 'You must have known what you were undertaking.'

She put her elbows on the table and cupped her chin in her hands and gave me a long, intent look.

'You fascinate me,' she said slowly.

'I do?'

'You do. There's something about you ... you look so *happy!*' she said in despair. 'Not outside. Inside.'

'What's wrong with looking happy inside?' asked Lindy.

'Well—' She leaned back in her chair and turned to Lindy. 'I don't see any *reason!* Look at her: she's a widow, and her children have left her and gone halfway across the world, and she has to work and she hasn't any money behind her, and she doesn't seem interested in men and she kills, stone dead, every smart gown that's put on her, and she lives in two ghastly rooms—they must be ghastly if they're over a shop—and ...' She frowned, and went on to me: 'I don't mind people being contented with their lot when they've got a lot. And I don't mind that serene look of yours in one way—I mean, if you're happy, that's fine—but why be happy before you've put out your hand and grabbed what nature's equipped you to grab? You could have so much! You could find a man and you could marry him and see that he looks after you. That's what men are for!'

I was on the point of asking her why she hadn't married again, and then changed my mind. I had seen her look at Alec Walsh—a brief but revealing look thrown across the room last night—a look that had met with no response. I said nothing.

'What you need,' she was saying, 'is a husband.'

'God forbid,' I said, and it was a prayer.

'Why?' asked Lindy. 'Weren't you happy with your husband?'

'Lyrically. But again—at this age? Over my dead body.'

A waiter appeared. Lindy and I disappeared behind the largest menus I had ever seen; when we had chosen and reappeared, Athena was still brooding.

'I'll have an entirely protein meal,' she said. 'They tell me protein repairs the body tissues—and after this morning, mine need repairing.'

She chose her food, and the waiter went away and then, quite without warning, Lindy looked across the table and spoke quietly.

'Mrs Rodrigues, did you take Mrs Verney's passport out of her bag?'

Athena scarcely hesitated, but I saw her cheeks whiten under her make-up.

'Yes,' she said. 'But if you want to know why I did, I can't tell you. You might understand—or you might not.'

Lindy looked relieved.

'I thought you were going to say that it wasn't my business.'

'Of course it's your business,' said Athena. 'If you didn't interest yourself in everything that was going on around you at this time, you'd be a fool—and you're no fool. For nineteen, you're quite a girl, and I'll tell you something else: you're the only girl I've ever come across who made me wish I'd had a daughter.'

'Thank you.'

'Don't thank me. You didn't see the ones I was comparing you with. Another question coming; what is it?'

'Why,' asked Lindy, 'does everybody in my father's firm seem to dislike everybody else in it?'

Athena stared across at her; at that moment she looked almost haggard.

'Is it so obvious?' she asked.

She was looking at me as she spoke, and she seemed to be waiting for an answer.

'If you mean can I feel it, too,' I said slowly, 'the answer is yes. There's some sort of ... undercurrent. I thought it could be explained by the fact that Mr Barron was missing. But he came back, and the tension was still there, and that's what Lindy wants explained—if you can explain it.'

'Why—' she turned to Lindy—'why don't you ask your father anything you want to know?'

'He wouldn't be able to tell me why you took Mrs Verney's passport out of her bag, would he?'

'No. No, he wouldn't.' Athena leaned forward, arms resting on the table, and spoke in an absent voice. 'And perhaps he wouldn't be able to explain the atmosphere in the office either. We're all—I think we're all waiting for something to ... to happen.'

'What sort of thing?' asked Lindy.

'Anything. We're just waiting, that's all. A little while ago, things between us all were smooth enough, on the surface. Now they're all tense, all wrong. All I know is that it dates from the time Alec and Cunha came back from that accursed trip to London.'

'To interview Charles Essex?'

'Yes. They went away on good enough terms, but they had a quarrel over the appointment.'

'Why?'

'It's a long story,' said Athena. 'They went over to make the final selection. The office in London had done the preliminary screening, and they'd left the final choice to Alec and Cunha. When they got to London, they didn't have to think twice: Essex was far and away the best man for the job. The idea was that if he turned out well, he'd be offered a junior partnership—eventually. That was why Searle was brought out, but Searle ... he wasn't all your father hoped he'd be, and so he decided to bring out another man. Neil Harper spoke to him about Essex, and your father wrote to the London office to ask them to have a close look at him; they did, and sent out a good report. So when Alec and Cunha chose him, everybody was satisfied. But when they made him the offer, Essex accepted—under certain conditions.'

We waited; food was brought and placed

before us, but we had lost interest in food.

'It turned out,' went on Athena presently, 'that Charles Essex had a rather strange history.'

'What sort of strange history?' asked Lindy.

Athena spoke quietly.

'His father was murdered,' she said.

'M—murdered!'

Lindy brought out the word on a note of horror, and I felt myself trembling. Murder seemed close to us all. It was no longer an affair of headlines or newspaper columns. It was close, and personal—and threatening.

'It happened a long time ago,' Athena went on. 'Eleven years ago.'

'Eleven years.' Lindy was calculating. 'And he's twenty-six, Neil said. So he was ... he was about fifteen when his father was—'

'Yes,' said Athena. 'Perhaps he wouldn't have told Alec and Cunha about it in the ordinary course of events. Neil Harper had said nothing. Essex himself had said nothing in the earlier interviews, and he might not have said anything later, but they wanted him in a hurry; he was to come out almost at once. When they told him that, he accepted the job, told them his story and said that he must be free to come to England at any time if the police sent for him.'

'Police!' I repeated.

'Yes. His stepmother had been tried for the murder of her husband, and she had been

130

acquitted. After the trial, she and her stepson, Charles, went to live abroad. He was at school in England, but he had no home there until he returned after her death. She died a year ago, and when Charles was going through her papers, he found some letters which he thought might interest the police. He brought them over to England. The police, after examining them, told him that they were going to follow up new evidence—something involving a foreigner. If they find out anything, he wants, naturally, to go to England to see them.'

'Yes, I can see that,' said Lindy. 'But why did Mr Walsh and Mr Cunha quarrel?'

'Because Cunha said they'd engage him under those conditions, and Alec said no. Cunha said that nobody was to be blamed because somebody murdered his father when he was about fourteen—but Alec took the line that it would be no use bringing into the firm a young man who had half his mind on his work and the other half on policemen and clues. He was adamant. He said the background was wrong. He said the news would leak out and wouldn't do the firm any good—besides which, there'd be investigators all over the place making nuisances of themselves.' She sighed. 'And for once,' she said, 'I'm against Alec. I can see his point of view, but I admit that in this affair, I'm on Cunha's side.'

'So they quarreled?' I asked.

'Yes. Cunha rang up Mr Barron. He
131

telephoned from London to Lisbon and explained the circumstances and got him to agree to having Charles Essex in the firm. So he's coming out, and in some way the appointment has had an effect on every one of us. Before, we were just a bunch of people who got along because we had one big interest—the firm—in common. I'm not saying we were good friends; I'm saying we got along; we were on good terms. Now ... we're not. Something's changed.'

I would have given a lot to ask her, at that moment, if she knew that an attempt had been made on Mr Barron's life. It seemed incredible that Lindy and I should know, and Alec and—I was certain—Cunha, and yet Athena be unaware of it. But I could not question her.

'When you come to think of it,' she said broodingly, 'you can see that the appointment of Essex was bound to cause trouble. Alec's furious because Cunha went over his head and phoned Bill Barron. Cunha was furious anyway, because Bill refused to have his brother in the firm. Searle knows perfectly well that Essex, like Neil Harper, will leave him well behind in the firm. And Searle can be dangerous. God knows what'll happen.'

'What could happen?' asked Lindy.

'Anything. I told you—Searle can be dangerous.' She stared at us through narrowed, brooding eyes. 'Dangerous? No. Not dangerous—but vindictive. He likes trouble, and we all know it—and that's why we've all got this awful feeling that when Essex arrives, Searle will make trouble. And with William Barron out of the way,' she went on slowly, 'there'd be plenty of trouble. Cunha would fight to get his brother into the firm. Neil Harper would line himself up against Alec, on the side of Essex. Alec and Searle ... well, they never got on, anyway. Yes, there'd be trouble—and Searle would help it along. And when he'd got all the other dogs fighting, he'd pick up the bone.'

'But ... why did you call him dangerous?' Lindy asked.

'Because he was trained to be dangerous. Robert Searle—Don't you—No, you won't know the name; you're too young.' She turned to me. 'You must remember it? Robert Searle. The young man who was decorated after the war for his work in enemy territory. Surely you remember?'

'Searle ... Searle.' I searched my memory, and forgotten headlines began to emerge. 'Searle ... yes, I do remember.'

'But that's ages and ages ago!' said Lindy.

'It was. But Searle isn't like most men,' said Athena. 'He hasn't put the war behind him. And he isn't like most heroes; he likes nothing better than to talk of his exploits. He isn't the only man in the firm who did a commendable war job; Alec and your father went through the war together, and I'll guarantee they did as much damage as Searle did—but they don't talk about it, and Searle does. He talks about the number of kills he made ... and how he made them.'

'Is there—' Lindy hesitated and then plunged on—'is there anything between Mr Searle and Mrs Cunha?'

'Since you ask me—yes; I think so,' said Athena. 'She's bored with her husband, and lately she and Searle ... I don't know. I don't think that even a trouble-maker like Searle would risk making an enemy of a man like Cunha. Cunha may look harmless enough, but if he thought anybody was going too far with his wife, he wouldn't hesitate before taking strong measures. In his way, he could be as dangerous as Searle. Your father knows all this, but he ... he doesn't care. Since we seem to have come out well into the open, I'll tell you this: I think your father is the most insensitive man God ever created. And he doesn't possess one spark of what's called nervous imagination. Fear is a thing that checks most people—but not your father. No, not him.'

She fell silent, and we finished the meal without another word. I sat thinking of all she had told us, and wondering what lay behind it. Somewhere, I felt, was a link connecting the bewildering sequence of events—or a key that would open a door. For the moment, there was nothing in my mind but confusion.

We left the restaurant and stood on the

pavement waiting for a taxi.

'I can't thank you enough,' I said to Athena. 'You've been very kind.'

'What have I done?' she asked.

I might have attempted to tell her, but at that moment I felt Lindy's hand on my arm. Following the direction of her glance, I saw that she was watching a man who was crossing the busy street—and limping. I recognized him as the man who had waited for Senhor Cunha near the café.

I longed to point him out to Athena, but I knew I could not do so without disregarding Senhor Cunha's plea for secrecy. But I saw that Lindy was determined to know who the man was, and with the intention of getting him into Athena's view, was pointing to a shop near the point at which he would step onto the pavement.

'May we look?' she asked, strolling towards the window.

'Only for a moment; here's a taxi,' said Athena.

A moment was enough. The man stepped onto the pavement an arm's length away from us. He saw Athena and bowed; she nodded in response.

'Who was that man?' asked Lindy, when we were in the taxi.

'The lame one, do you mean?'

'Yes.'

'He's Luis Cunha's brother, Fernando.'

135

'Is he the one—'

'Your father wouldn't have in the firm? Yes.'

I stared out of the window and tried to assemble my thoughts. But nothing seemed to be clear except the fact that Fernando Cunha, who had not been invited to join Mr Barron's firm, had led his brother Luis to a meeting place in a hut on a piece of waste ground—and if this fact were known, Mr Barron would be in danger. For the rest, all was a haze; Searle was dangerous, Cunha was resentful, Athena had stolen my passport and hadn't told us why, Sylvana was indiscreet or worse, and William Barron...

Once before—on the *Juan Cortez*—I had resolved to put Mr Barron and his affairs out of my mind. I had kept to my resolution then, and I would keep it now.

And for almost three hours, I did.

CHAPTER SIX

I didn't see any of the Barrons until the evening. Mr Barron had spent the morning at his office; Rex had gone sight-seeing. When Lindy and I got home after lunching with Athena, I went to my room to rest, and Lindy got out her paints and brushes and settled herself on a branch of a large tree in the middle of the garden, painting a picture of the house.

At the end of two or three hours, she came to me to exhibit the results of this labor: a somewhat Impressionist view of the house and, on the back of her dress, an almost equally picturesque effect, in three colors.

'I can identify the blotches on the canvas,' I told her. 'But if you wanted to do a reproduction on your dress, why on the back? Why not on the front?'

Lindy screwed herself around to examine the damage.

I spilt three of the colors,' she explained.

'And then you sat on them?'

'I suppose.'

'Well, both pictures are charming,' I told her.

She grinned.

'I'll go and change. Father's taking Rex and I for a sight-seeing drive.'

'Rex and *myself*.'

'Wrong. Rex and *me*,' she threw at me from the door.

As I was dressing for dinner, she came into my room, already dressed, and sat on my bed.

'Feel rested?' she asked.

'Yes, thank you. Lindy—'

She smiled.

'I know what you're going to say, but go ahead and say it,' she said.

'Why did you ... when did you think that Athena had taken my passport?'

'I hadn't thought about her at all—in that

connection,' said Lindy. 'But when we were sitting at the table, I began to think of times and places, and I remembered your movements before the passport was lost—and I remembered your saying that you'd gone to let Alec Walsh in. And you probably didn't take your bag with you. I thought that if I asked Athena straight out, without warning... and it worked, you see. Only—she didn't tell us why.'

'No. And lying here this afternoon, I decided I wasn't going to spoil my last days here playing the detective. Honestly, Lindy, I wouldn't have said I was a dull-witted woman, but ... I can't make head nor tail. And I'm not going to try to. Couldn't we talk about something else—something unconnected with murder?'

'Yes. A party,' said Lindy. 'Daddy's giving one for us tomorrow evening—a big one. He arranged it before we arrived; it's a sort of welcome.'

'Tomorrow evening? Isn't it tomorrow evening that Charles Essex arrives?'

'Yes. But his plane doesn't get in until fairly late, so he'll miss the beginning.'

'Is Neil coming?'

A shadow fell across her face.

'Daddy said he'd been invited, but he said that Neil never accepts his invitations if he can get out of them. I wish ... I wish they liked one another more.'

I didn't like to point out that as far as I could see, Mr Barron was prepared to be friendly enough; it was Neil who drew back.

'Of course he'll come,' I said. 'I hope so, anyway; he'll be someone I can talk to. We'll ask him about it when he comes this evening.'

Neil arrived; we asked him about it and learned that he had every intention of being present at the party. No sooner had this point been settled, than Mr Barron appeared and led him into the study.

'Won't keep him long,' he promised Lindy and myself. 'You can come, too, if you want to.'

'Is it private?' asked Lindy.

'Yes,' said her father. 'But as you both know so much already, you'd better know a bit more.'

We went into the room in which Lindy and I had seen Sylvana. Mr Barron poured drinks for us all, and then looked at Neil and came straight to the point.

'I'm going to talk about your friend Essex, and I want frank answers,' he said. 'And in case you feel that it isn't any concern of the ladies, let me inform you that they both spent the morning worming the firm's secrets out of Athena. So now we can go on. When you recommended Essex to me,' he went on, 'you said nothing about a murder.'

'No, sir.'

'All right; you felt that it was old history and

not to be dragged out. Perhaps you were right. But when you were on leave, you must have known that the case had come into the news again?'

'Yes, I did.'

'And so you must have discussed it with your father, because your father was the judge who tried the case—right?'

'Yes, sir.'

'Will you agree that although I may not have had the right to ask questions about Essex before, the fact that he's now a member of my firm gives me a certain right to question you now?'

'Yes,' agreed Neil.

'Especially as you're aware,' went on Mr Barron, 'that his appointment has stirred up a lot of trouble.'

'I know that Mr Walsh opposed the appointment, sir.' Neil frowned. 'I don't know if he had any reason for his attitude, apart from—'

'Apart from thinking that the background was undesirable? If he had, he didn't take me into his confidence,' said Mr Barron dryly. 'What I would like to learn from you is your father's view of the case. I know nothing beyond the fact that the father of Essex was murdered and—well, you take it on from there.'

'His father was murdered, and his stepmother was tried for the murder,' said

Neil. 'My father became convinced, during the trial, that she was innocent. He was certain that she had not committed the murder, and he was also certain that she knew who had killed her husband.'

'But she said nothing?'

'Nothing. My father said he felt that she was waiting—she knew the murderer, and was waiting for him, or her, to come forward. But nobody came forward, and my father said that it was only by God's mercy and his summing up that she didn't hang.'

'You mean,' said Mr Barron, 'that someone murdered her husband and let her—'

'Go close to hanging for it. Yes,' said Neil.

I glanced at Lindy. She was looking from one man to the other, and there seemed to me to be as much pride and love in her eyes when she looked at Neil as when her gaze rested on her father. She was proud of her father, and I could see why: he had good looks and strength and confidence and a rather overriding brand of charm. But she could be proud of Neil, too, for there were not many young men who could stand so easily, so quietly and with such dignity before Mr Barron and his curt, brusque questions.

'What I wanted to get from you,' Mr Barron was saying, 'was some idea of the facts of the case. You know that there has been a difference of opinion about the appointment of Essex; I had to have something to go on.'

'I'd like to say, sir, that I feel strongly that Charles can't be held—'

'Nobody's going to hold him,' broke in Mr Barron. 'Or hold him responsible, if that's what you were going to say. There's new evidence coming up, isn't there?'

'Charles found some letters among his mother's papers, and he took them to the police. I understand they're looking for somebody, and if they find him—'

'Well, I hope they do,' said Mr Barron. 'And as far as the firm's concerned, our sympathies will be with Essex. I hope they catch the man or woman who did it.' He took Neil's glass and refilled it. 'I hope they catch the swine. I hope they make him sorry he left that poor devil of a woman to take the rap. I don't mind a straightforward murder. It's something I might do myself, given sufficient provocation. Murder's one thing—but leaving a woman to go through hell in a criminal court, leaving her to—well, I hope they catch the swine and string him up.'

'Ladies present,' Lindy reminded him.

'Neither of them shock easily, thank God,' he said. 'Oh—' He turned to the desk, pulled open a drawer, took out a large envelope and dropped it onto my lap. 'Steamer ticket. Cabin on the *Princesa Isabel*, leaving three days from now. I wish it weren't so soon, but I know you're anxious to go. This time—' he grinned—'it's a single berth cabin; no chance

142

of getting into trouble. And in the presence of witnesses, let me say that I'm grateful to you, more grateful than I can say.'

'I haven't done anything,' I said in surprise. 'Except act like a lunatic and lose my ship.'

'You were around,' said Mr Barron, 'when you were needed. That's more than you can say for most people. I'll fix up your passport before you go.'

'You needn't,' I told him. 'It came back in the post this morning.'

'It ... it what?'

'It was posted back to me.'

'Who the devil—'

'Never mind who,' broke in Lindy swiftly. 'It's back.' She looked at her father. 'Daddy—'

'Well?'

'Could Aunt Kate and I talk frankly to Neil about everything that has happened here? Or would you rather we didn't?'

'I'd rather you did,' he said without hesitation. 'He's guessed already that somebody'd prefer me dead. If there's any more, go ahead and tell him. We need a cool observer—and did you ever see anything as cool as he is? Tell him, and see if his inherited legal brain can get to work. And have a good dinner and don't come home late.'

He opened the door and strolled to the front door with us; Lindy and Neil walked ahead, and I followed with Mr Barron and found him looking down at me with a grin.

143

'Know something?' he said. 'I—'

'You took both your children out today and you let Rex drive the car for part of the way and you behaved like a model parent—to both of them. If I had a trumpet, I'd blow it for you. Good night.'

I caught up with the other two and found myself once more in the gray car, this time with less room, for Lindy was seated between Neil and myself. We left the quiet street and went down to the noisy city and stopped at a restaurant not far from the Rossio; the street was unpretentious and the entrance uninviting, but when we were inside, I saw that we were going to eat well—and expensively.

Neil did not look at the menu; he waited silently, his eyes on Lindy, while we chose and rejected and chose again. Then he asked if he might have the pleasure of choosing for us; ten seconds later, the waiter was going in the direction of the kitchen and Neil was looking across the table at us.

'Quite like old times,' he remarked, and smiled at me. 'You didn't have any premonitions on board—why?'

'I was never psychic,' I told him. 'That's why I can't guess why Athena stole my passport. But don't let's talk about it until we've had our wonderful dinner. I've been put off one meal today.'

So it was not until the end of the meal that we told Neil all that had happened, and told him without reserve. We told him everything we knew of the attempt on Mr Barron's life, about Sylvana in the study, about Athena and the passport and even about Luis Cunha and his brother Fernando. Lindy did most of the telling, and she kept the account as impersonal as possible. She gave him the facts baldly, and when she had finished, I poured out our coffee and we leaned back and prepared to listen to his comments.

He didn't speak for some time. He stirred his coffee and smoked his cigarette thoughtfully.

'Well?' asked Lindy at last.

His first words were addressed to me.

'Your brother Henry,' he said, 'would have pointed out to you at this stage how easily you could have kept out of trouble. You should have gone away on the *Juan Cortez*.'

'But I didn't.'

'No. I suppose you realize that you're very close to danger?'

'I'm in the room across the hall from Mr Barron, and somebody's anxious to kill him; I suppose you could call that close. Lindy's close to danger, too—and so is Rex.'

'And their father,' said Neil, 'should send them both away.'

'I wouldn't go,' said Lindy.

'Then he should put the whole matter,' said Neil, 'into the hands of the police.'

'He won't,' said Lindy, and Neil smiled.

'No, he won't. Of course he won't,' he said.

'The businessman veneer is very thin. Your father's a born fighter, and he's enjoying himself more now, I'd say, than he has done since the war. Somebody's out to get him; he's a target, and he thinks—he hopes—he'll have a chance to come to grips. But he won't. You can tell him that from me when you go home, and you can post me my dismissal.'

'Why did Athena steal Aunt Kate's passport?'

'To keep her here, of course.' He threw me a bland look. 'Distraction without competition. Athena's got her hands full of her own special troubles at the moment. If Mrs Verney had gone away and if your father had come to any harm, she was the obvious person to have you and Rex—and she didn't want that because she's got her hands too full at the moment.'

'Why?' asked Lindy.

Neil hesitated.

'Because she's having a last try at—'

'At?'

'At getting Alec Walsh to marry her.'

Lindy and I had nothing to say; our minds were busy with this new slant.

'She wants to marry Walsh,' Neil went on. 'She's been doing her best to bring it off for some time, but she won't succeed. I happen to know that he's hoping to marry the daughter of a fellow in the Embassy, and I think the engagement will be announced soon. She's younger than Alec by some years, this girl, but she's attractive. And so is he.' He looked at Lindy. 'I think your father had a hand in it; he was never keen on seeing Alec tied to Athena, and I don't blame him. She's not a nice character.'

Nice character or not, I found myself unaccountably depressed on Athena's account. To love Walsh and to lose him ... that was bad enough. To lose him to a chit from the Embassy...

Passion, I reflected, did odd things to men. I stared at my mental picture of Alec Walsh and found that it had got faintly out of focus. Young girls were for young men. I couldn't reconcile my impressions of Alec Walsh with this new idea of him as a man preparing to marry a girl who sounded young enough to be his daughter. And Athena...

'I like Athena,' I said. 'She was kind to me.'

'That's because all she wanted out of you was your passport—and she'd helped herself to it.'

'Why didn't Senhor Cunha want us to tell the others about his meeting with his brother?' asked Lindy.

'I don't know. But I'd like to know and I propose to ask him.'

'I like him,' I said.

'Cunha?'

'Yes. At first I didn't, but there's something about him—'

'Like Athena?'

'No.' I leaned forward and spoke urgently. 'Neil,' I said, 'somebody is trying to kill Mr Barron. We've told you all we know about it, and we hoped ... I hoped you'd make some sense of it all.'

'What makes you think I haven't?'

'Because you've said nothing to clear up any of the confusion. I hoped you'd get all the tangles out of my mind.'

'Nobody can do that. You've got your facts inextricably mixed with your people. To see a way through this, you have to be able to study facts without relation to personalities—and you're not capable of doing that,' he said gently. 'When you're in someone's company, you don't use your head; you use ... feelers. You'll never make a detective, if that's what you're trying to be, because you're not interested in impersonalities, if I may use the word.'

'But couldn't you try and make us see what's going on?' asked Lindy.

'If you wait a couple of days, I don't think you'll need me to tell you.'

'I don't understand.'

'This is murder in a hurry,' said Neil. 'I know, at this moment, nothing definite about who or why, but one fact emerges clearly; someone is trying to get rid of your father quickly. That is all I know for certain tonight. Tomorrow, I'll begin asking questions; I may find the answers or I may not.'

We sat staring at him, and I knew that nothing that had happened up to now had brought the situation home to me with the force and horror of his quiet, unemphatic words. Murder. And not murder attempted or murder averted—but murder to come.

I had nothing to say. All bewilderment, all curiosity had faded from my mind. I didn't want to know any more; I wanted to know less.

I saw the bill brought. I saw Neil examine it. He paid it and sat looking at us for a few moments 'And now you understand,' he said to me at last, 'why people who have your welfare at heart wish that you had gone away on the *Juan Cortez*. Great mistake, missing that boat.' He looked at his watch and then across at us. 'I got three tickets for the theater,' he told us. 'Would you care to go? Ballet.'

I shook myself out of my gloom.

'Thank you. I'd like it very much. But won't you and Lindy—'

'Not without you,' said Lindy firmly. 'Hurry up. I adore ballet.'

'Nice music,' said Neil.

'And nice dancing,' she added.

'Don't know about that. Find it all very soothing,' said Neil. 'I close my eyes and listen to the music and the swish-swish on the stage. Very restful.'

He seemed to be asleep through the entire performance. In the two intervals he woke up and—after my refusal to accompany them—

shepherded Lindy out to the foyer and then brought her back again and relapsed into thoughtfulness. I felt that only part of him was in the theater; the other half was far away, and wherever the place was, I knew it had some connection with William Barron and the attempt on his life. Neil had absorbed all that we had told him and he was turning it over in his mind; when he had thought it over, he might have a theory—but if he had, I didn't think that we would be able to get it out of him. If he arrived at any conclusion, he wouldn't tell us what it was—yet.

He opened his eyes at the end of the performance, asked us what we were waiting for and explained that they didn't play 'God Save the Queen' at the end of Lisbon shows. He took us to his flat, and a fat, cheerful little maid gave us coffee and sandwiches. The place was small, but there was an enclosed veranda and we stood looking out at the lights of the city and listening to the noise of the traffic. Lindy looked relaxed and at ease, and I felt in some way strengthened; Neil Harper had done us good, even if he had left our curiosity unsatisfied. He had unraveled no mysteries, untied no knots.

'You really believe,' said Lindy out of a long silence, 'that he's in danger?'

'Your father? I'd say that he's in grave and imminent danger. Someone wants to kill him, and kill him soon. Tell him that from me.'

'Could it be because—' She hesitated. 'Could it be because of ... of those scandals?'

'No.'

'How can you be so sure?'

'Because nothing of that sort has happened lately. People don't brood on matters of that kind and then suddenly decide to revenge themselves—not as a rule, anyhow. A jealous man—in this country—would kill in hot and not in cold blood. This thing, as your father seems to realize, is in some way unrelated to his past indiscretions.'

'Could it be anybody in ... in the firm?' I asked.

'Why not? When you're looking for a murderer, you're looking in strange places. You might say that each one of them had a motive. Except Alec Walsh, perhaps. Of them all, he's the one you'd have most difficulty in fitting into a murderer's frame. But the others? How does anybody know? Cunha wanted to bring his brother into the firm; he told me—he told everybody—that Barron had given him reason to think it could be arranged. But when it came to the point, Mr Barron refused. That doesn't seem a reason for wanting to kill a man, but we don't know what's behind it. Searle has been supplanted by Charles; again not a reason for murder, but Searle has a reputation for recklessness. Sylvana? Athena? You can rule them out, I imagine.'

'Why?' asked Lindy. 'Because a woman

couldn't have fixed that wire?'

'No.' He smiled down at her and spoke gently. 'No. Because I don't think a woman would want to kill your father.'

I was silent, but it was not the silence of agreement. I myself thought that under certain circumstances, a woman might be very happy to kill William Barron. I would have given a great deal to know what Sylvana had been looking for on his desk. If we knew that ... but neither Mr Walsh nor Neil had seemed to feel that the incident had any special significance.

'What are you brooding over?' Neil asked me presently.

'About Sylvana Cunha. I was wondering what she was looking for on Mr Barron's desk.'

'It doesn't matter—much—what she was looking for. All that's important is the fact that she was looking for it.'

'But she—'

'Are you being a detective again? You wouldn't,' he said gently, 'make a good one.'

'Why not?' I demanded.

'Why wouldn't she?' Lindy asked curiously.

'Because—' he answered her question— 'because she would give the whole show away.'

'She wouldn't!' Lindy sprang hotly to my defense. 'She wouldn't say a word.'

He laughed. 'She would be discretion itself—as far as words went. But her face would give her away. Don't you see?'

152

They both studied me. I tried to look as expressionless as possible, but the attempt must have been unsuccessful, for presently Lindy bent and dropped a light kiss on my nose.

'Yes, I see,' she told him.

'If you've both finished—' I began.

'It's your eyes,' said Lindy. 'They're ... they're truthful eyes.'

'They're frank eyes,' said Neil. 'She would look at the murderer—and he would know that she knew.'

'Well, why were Sylvana and Searle taking something off Mr Barron's desk?' I asked him.

'They were in all probability going through his morning's mail, which he hadn't seen. They were taking something out of it. Why? Because they were afraid that someone else was going to deal with that mail. Alec Walsh, or Cunha, or ... Mr Barron's executors.'

'Executors?' Lindy's voice was suddenly shaky.

'You don't imagine, do you,' Neil asked her, 'that Alec Walsh is the only one who knows that an attempt was made on your father's life?'

'He's the only one my father told. How would the others know?'

'Cunha's news came, most likely, through his brother Fernando. Searle, and therefore Sylvana, would know about the wire.'

'You mean they ... they saw it?'

'I'm pretty certain Searle must have seen it—if he didn't put it there. The most natural thing in the world would have been for Searle to get into his car when your father didn't turn up to meet the boat, and drive out to see if he could locate him in the places he always rides in every morning. I think Searle did that. I think he drove out there and I think he saw the wire—and he went back and said nothing. If a man comes across a clear attempt at murder, and decides to keep his mouth shut, he's got one of two reasons for doing so: he's afraid for himself, or he's afraid for somebody else.'

So I had been right, I thought. Below their anxiety for Mr Barron's safety, beneath their expressions of worry and suspense, I had seen fear—and now I knew the reason. They had all known—and said nothing.

I found myself thinking of each of them in a new way. Alec Walsh must have guessed a good deal; below his quiet manner there had been the knowledge that his oldest friend was in danger. I felt sorry for him; William Barron, I knew, would not be an easy man to reason with. Athena ... For a moment I forgot her kindness and remembered her cool, calculating theft of my passport. I forgot Senhor Cunha's unexpectedly attractive smile and saw him only as an unloved husband with a wife he could not trust. I saw Sylvana bending furtively over the desk, with Searle—who had killed and boasted of his killing—waiting for her outside. I saw—

154

'Are you sorry you left home?' I heard Neil say.

'If you mean do I enjoy sitting on a time bomb—no,' I told them. 'I don't think I ever wanted excitement, even of the milder kind. And this kind ... no. But even my brother would have to admit that I didn't go looking for it. I shared a cabin with a girl and became friendly with her and with her brother. They came to me when their father was missing, and I couldn't have refused to go back to the house with them, could I? Or to stay with them until the boat sailed. After that, things weren't in my hands—my passport vanished and I was stuck.'

Neil turned to Lindy with a smile. 'She got into this for one reason only,' he told her, 'and that is because every time she sees a girl like you she adopts her. She becomes a possessive, protective mother. Her troubles began when you knocked her brother flying and hurtled into the train. From the beginning of it all, she was emotionally engaged and now here she is, in the middle of it—and I'm glad that she is. Whatever risks your father takes on his own account are his own affair, but I don't think I could have an easy moment if you and Rex didn't have somebody to ... to lean on.'

We stood there for a long time, saying nothing; then I said, reluctantly, that it was time we were going.

He put Lindy's fur around her shoulders—

Athena had suggested my buying one, but after a short struggle with my conscience, I had decided that there was no need for Barron & Walsh to give me an evening wrap; I had a perfectly good one on the *Juan Cortez* and I would probably catch up with it one day. I hoped so; Henry's wife had given it to me; it was an old one of hers, and when she gave away something she didn't want, she kept a strict check to see that you were using it. If you weren't, she took it back.

We drove to the big house on the hill; the city's winking lights dropped behind us. We scarcely spoke; we had turned into the drive of the *Casa Roma* before Neil spoke again.

'Lights on in the house,' he said to Lindy. 'That means someone's up. If it's your father, tell him what I've told you about going to the police and giving them the whole story.'

The car stopped; he handed us out.

'Thank you both for coming,' he said. 'Been a great pleasure.' He took Lindy's hand, and I walked away and pretended to be looking for something in my handbag. Then the car had gone and Lindy was beside me.

'If father's up, will you come with me to talk to him?' she asked.

'I will,' I said resolutely.

And I would have, if at that moment the door behind us hadn't opened with a rush and Rex, deathly pale, hadn't seized my arm and dragged me inside and towards the stairs.

'It's ...' Rex shuddered. 'It's Daddy. He's hurt. Do come quickly, please!'

'Is he ...' I stopped.

'Please come!' urged Rex.

With my heart in my new shoes, I followed them upstairs.

CHAPTER SEVEN

Mr Barron was lying half in, half out of his bedroom; the upper part of his body was on the balcony, and scattered around the floor was a mass of broken glass; I saw that the panels of the door were shattered. A patch of blood stained the shoulder of Mr Barron's pajamas, and there was a red weal running down one of his cheeks.

I dropped to my knees beside him, and Lindy rushed to the medicine chest. Rex held back the pajama coat and we went to work with cotton wool and lint. Nobody spoke; Lindy's lips trembled, but her hands were firm. Rex, white and disheveled, looked as though he had leapt hastily from his bed.

In a few moments, Mr Barron sat up. Then, without a word, he got to his feet; he looked shaken, and I thought that he must have fallen very heavily. He walked slowly to his chair and slumped into it, and Lindy mopped at the blood that was still coming from the wound on his shoulder.

'That'll need stitches,' I told him, and he nodded.

'Rex phoned the doctor,' he said.

I was afraid to ask what had happened. Mr Barron looked at me, and all I saw in his eyes was black anger; his lips were set in a grim and bitter line. He nodded towards the broken glass; he made a grimace and spoke in a tone that he meant to make reassuring.

'All my own fault,' he said. 'Went out onto the balcony for a bit of air and didn't realize the door had shut behind me. Came back and walked clean through it—almost.'

He spoke with an effort that I felt was mental as well as physical; Lindy smiled at him, but when I glanced at Rex, I saw to my dismay that his father's words had brought no change to his sick, set young face. I wondered whether he had been forming his own horrifying conclusions.

We waited, for the most part in silence, until the doctor came; then I left Lindy to help him and went out. I saw that Rex had followed me and was shutting the door behind him.

'Aunt Kate—' He stopped and made a visible effort at self-control. 'I ...' Once again he stopped, and I took his arm and led him into my room.

'What is it?' I asked.

'My father—'

'He'll be all right. He isn't badly hurt.'

'It isn't that. What he said about … about how it happened … it wasn't true. He said it for Lindy, I suppose.' He paused and pulled himself together. 'It was a knife.'

'A … a knife!' I did my best to keep my voice steady, but I knew that I spoke with a quaver. 'But Rex—'

'It was a knife. It was … it was thrown from outside. From the garden.' He stared at me with horror-filled eyes. 'Somebody wanted to … to kill him. Somebody wanted to kill him—wanted to kill my father. They did, didn't they?'

'Yes,' I said, and saw the look of gratitude on his face. 'But look, Rex—'

He shook his head and drew a deep breath.

'I was afraid you might try to put me off,' he said. 'Does Lindy—'

'Lindy knows. I wouldn't worry too much if I were you, Rex. Your father is a very rich and important and influential man, and people like that always have the odd lunatic trying to harm them—venting their jealousy.'

He took no notice of my feeble comfort; I don't think he even heard it.

'Yesterday—that accident. Was that … did they—'

'Yes,' I said. 'Your father tried to keep it from you both, but Lindy guessed a little and made him tell her what had happened. What happened tonight?'

'Dad and I stayed up rather late, and I

played him all the records we'd brought out. It was a ... a good evening; we had a lot of fun. Then we had coffee and sandwiches and came up to bed and talked for a bit in Dad's room and then we sort of drifted off to bed. But I didn't go straight to sleep; it was the coffee, I suppose; usually I just go off like the dead. I thought some aspirin might send me off, and I got up to ask Dad for some. I came along the corridor and I ... I heard a crash and I heard Dad give a sort of ... it wasn't a ... cry, exactly, and I rushed in and that was how I saw what had happened. The—' He stopped and I saw a shudder go through him. 'The knife was in his shoulder and he ... he took it out and told me to get it out of sight quickly in case you and Lindy came back and came in to see what was happening. Then I phoned for the doctor, but there didn't seem to be anything else that I could do—and then I heard you and Lindy come in.'

'There was something else you could have done,' I said, 'and I think you should do it now. Ring up Mr Walsh and ask him if he can come.'

'Yes—oh yes!' His face was eager. 'But ... won't he think it queer if we ask him to come like this in the middle of the night?'

'No, he won't; he'll want to be here with your father,' I said.

Rex went to the door and then turned and spoke slowly.

'Aunt Kate, about what happened

yesterday—'

'Well?'

'Does anybody know about it? Anybody but you and Lindy, I mean?'

'Mr Harper thinks that everybody knows—everybody in the office, that is. But Mr Walsh is the only one your father spoke to about it. And he told Lindy that we could tell Neil Harper.'

'And the ... the police?'

'Your father seemed to feel that, for the moment, he didn't want them. Mr Harper said it was madness, and so it was, but after tonight I don't think there'll be any question of not calling them in.'

'Why didn't Dad—'

'He had an idea that if anybody wanted him out of the way, they'd have another try at it. And the next time—he thought—he'd see trouble coming. But as you see, he didn't. I think he felt that once the police were on the job, you and Lindy would be mixed up in it, and he didn't want that. So if you could get Mr Walsh here and ask him to shout your father down and call in the police at once, I think it would be a good thing.'

Rex said nothing for a moment. He was standing with his eyes on mine and his thoughts far away.

'Whoever threw that knife,' he said slowly at last, 'must have thrown it from that tree.'

'Which tree?'

'The one Lindy climbed this morning, to get a view of the house when she was painting that picture of it. The big one in the center of the garden; it was the obvious one for anybody who wanted to be directly in front of the balcony...'

In the morning, a girl had climbed up into the branches with her paints and her brushes and her canvas; at night, somebody had gone up with a knife. I looked at Rex; his mouth was firm and he had his father's look of cool, steady purpose. I would have liked to have known what he was thinking, but without saying any more, he turned and went out of the room.

I sat down on a chair, feeling a little weak. We had driven to the front door less than twenty minutes ago. Neil had left us standing there in front of the house, and—and, good heavens!—at that very moment somebody was throwing knives at the other side of the house.

I shivered. I didn't feel at all like undressing and going to bed. Not in this house, anyhow. I wanted suddenly, more than anything else in the world, to be on the *Juan Cortez* in mid-Atlantic, with clean sea air all around me, and no dark memories of horses falling screaming to their death, and no knives coming hurtling through the night. This violence and horror had nothing to do with me; I was a quiet, unknown, undistinguished woman going peaceably about my own business, and all I had done was respond to the friendly overtures

162

of a couple of nice children. And for that, I was landed—landed was the word—with a set of people who would have been considered by Henry odd in the extreme—Athena and the Cunhas and Robert Searle—and in the room across from mine, at this moment, was a man who had twice in two days been the victim of what the newspapers called an outrage. I shuddered, and looked with relief at the closed door leading out to my own balcony. It wouldn't be a bad idea, I thought, to close the shutters, too.

I got up and I had taken two steps towards the door when I heard the soft, spattering sound—and the next thing I remember was finding myself cowering behind the bed with my hands over my head. It was a heroic pose, but I wasn't feeling heroic.

Then it came to me, terrified though I was, that I was behaving not only like a coward but like a fool. Murderers didn't throw tiny fragments of gravel up at a window; they threw rocks—or knives.

The sound came again—gentle, but unmistakable. Somebody was outside; somebody was down there—and somebody wanted me.

I closed my eyes and prayed that caution and not curiosity might be my guide, and then I went slowly to the door and opened it and walked out onto the balcony. If cowering beside the bed was a craven act, walking out

163

onto that balcony certainly was not.

I heard a hiss. Although I didn't yet know who was down there, I was grateful for the hiss, because it restored me to my normal frame of mind, which is one in which murderers have no place. The hiss, I considered, was pure melodrama.

I heard a sound behind me, and turned to find Lindy coming into the room. After one glance at my face, she came quickly to my side.

'You look—What is it?' she asked. 'You're so white. All this has upset you.'

'No. Somebody threw gravel up at the window.'

She stared at me.

'Somebody—'

We walked out and looked down and saw Sylvana Cunha.

She was wearing a long black cloak, and she was standing at the edge of the shadow; she was perfectly still, but her immobility told us better than any gestures that we were to make no sound.

We stood there for a few moments and then she raised a hand and pointed to one of the windows downstairs. It was the window of the study, and we understood that she wanted us to go down and let her in.

We went downstairs. After closing the study door, I snapped on the light, and Lindy opened the long window by which Sylvana had left the morning before. She came in and closed the shutters behind her; then she turned, and I saw that she was deathly pale. Then she addressed me.

'I have got to speak with you,' she said.

But at first she didn't do much speaking. She seemed about to begin, and then she had taken a few steps and put her head down on my shoulder and burst into tears—hard, racking, shaking sobs.

After the first moment of surprise, my arms went around her automatically, and there we stood. Even through her cloak I could feel the skin-and-boniness of her, and I thought of Sue, and I wanted to feed this fragile little thing up on plenty of nice, fattening starch. And she went on sobbing.

At last she stopped. She produced a tiny, lace-edged handkerchief, and with that and Lindy's wisp and my somewhat more sensible one we mopped up her tears. The front of my new evening dress was damp, and I didn't think the material would stand up to salt water, but I reminded myself that Sylvana had in an indirect way contributed to the purchase and so might have some right to drop tears on it.

'I had to come,' she said at last, and now she was speaking to Lindy. 'I had to.'

'What do you want?' asked Lindy gently.

Sylvana looked at us out of black, enormous eyes. She was all black eyes and cloak and hair and white face, standing there etched against the long curtains.

'I want the knife,' she said.

'The knife?' echoed Lindy.

Sylvana put out a trembling hand and took one of Lindy's.

'You know about it—ah, but you know! I saw you up there with ... with him. At first, I thought he was dead, and I was afraid—so much, so much afraid—and then I saw that you were with him and I—Please, Lindy, listen to me! I must have the knife!'

'Lindy can't give it to you,' I said. 'She hasn't got it. Rex was told by his father to put it out of sight before Lindy and I came in.'

'You must get it.' She had swung around to Lindy. 'You must give it to me. You are the only one who can do this. Your father will not give it up. He will keep it—or he will give it to the police. Either way, it will be ... it will be terrible. If you could understand what this means to me, you would not hesitate. I can only beg you ... beg you ...'

She stopped and turned to me. She seemed to be waiting for me to say something, but I had nothing to say. She looked old and haggard—and she was little more than a child.

'Do you know,' asked Lindy, 'who threw the knife?'

'No. I do not know. I swear to you that I do not know.'

'But you must know whose knife it is?'

'Yes. I know that. And that is why you must give it to me. I would not ask you to do anything that is wrong—believe me,' she begged. 'And you must believe me when I say that if you do not give me the knife, you will be harming a—an innocent person.'

I thought of Neil Harper's words; he had said that he did not think a woman would kill William Barron. I felt now that a woman might give some one else a reason for killing him.

'I haven't seen the knife,' said Lindy. 'I—'

She stopped. From the other side of the house there had come the sound of a car. Sylvana went swiftly across the room and switched off the light; I felt, rather than heard her beside me once more.

'It is Mr Walsh,' she whispered presently.

She had clutched my arm; now I felt her fingers gradually loosen their hold. There was something in the slow slackening that gave me an uncanny sense of hope draining out, slipping away. We stood there and heard the swift feet of Rex as he came down to let Alec in; we heard them go upstairs, and in the silence that followed, Sylvana walked across the room and switched on the light once more. The look on her face made my heart turn over.

'What is it? Oh, what is it?' I asked. 'You're so young. You've got all your life before you, and you're mixed up with ... with this—'

'With murder,' she said.

'But why—why?'

'One does not always seek. Things come— haven't you found that out, yesterday and today? Your passport—don't you know that Athena Rodrigues stole it?'

'Yes, I know.'

'And you? You know also?'

'Yes,' said Lindy.

'You were with her this morning. She perhaps told you many things, but how much was the truth? Did she tell you that she is in love with Alec Walsh? Do you know that she has always hoped to marry him? Did she tell you that she hates your father because he has great influence with Alec Walsh, and does not wish them to marry because he does not trust Athena? No, she would not tell you that, because all that is the truth. She would tell you, instead, that I am in love with Robert Searle. She would tell you that my husband is angry because your father did not have Fernando Cunha in the firm. She would tell you—'

Her voice was rising, and I heard my own breaking in on it.

'Mrs Cunha, why don't you go home—back to your husband? Why don't you keep out of this trouble, whatever it is? Go home and tell your husband and let him take care of you. You've got no business to be running about in the middle of the night looking for knives and talking about murder. Go home—and stay there.'

I heard my own impatience and exasperation and I suppose she heard it too. She pushed her hair back from her forehead and looked at me with tired eyes.

'I went home,' she said. 'And my husband ... wasn't there. So I came ...'

She stopped. For one moment, I thought she was going to faint. I led her to a chair and put her into it. When I tried to take my hand away, she caught it and held it and spoke in a low, rapid voice.

'Mrs Verney, I must tell somebody, or I shall go mad! But if I tell you, you will perhaps think that I am not speaking the truth and ... I need help! I need help so much, so much!'

I saw Lindy drop to her knees beside the other girl's chair and speak to her in a soft, infinitely soothing voice.

'What is it? Please tell me,' she said.

Sylvana looked at her.

'The knife. It is ... my husband's. But he did not—I swear to you that—No. I cannot swear it. I can only say that I believe with all my heart that he did not come here to hurt Mr Barron.'

'Hurt—You mean that he came here—with a knife?'

'I do not think that he came here. But he has a knife. It is kept, it has for as long as I remember been kept in a drawer in his desk— but it is not there any longer. I ask you to believe that my husband did not use it—but how will he explain? How can he explain that it is his, and that he did not use it?'

'Where is your husband now?' asked Lindy.

She shook her head despairingly.

169

'I don't know. At dinner tonight we ... we quarreled. He told me some things that he had heard about me. I asked him who said them, and he said—after some time—that it was Athena Rodrigues. And I ... I think I wanted to kill her. I drove to her house—but she was not there. So I went home, and when I got home, I found that my husband had gone ... and something, some fear made me look for the knife. It was not there. I was afraid, because I though that he might have believed what Athena had said about me and ... and your father. I came here and—'

'Were you out there when the knife was thrown?' I asked.

'No. No, I swear.' She turned to Lindy. 'I saw lights in the house, and I came around into the garden—and up there on your father's balcony, I saw you and your brother and Mrs Verney. You were all helping him ... he was hurt ... and I thought of the knife.'

'How do you know that the one thrown at my father—'

'A knife disappears. A knife is thrown. In this case, it is not—'

'What did your husband's knife look like?'

'It is not very long. It is ... it is thin, and it has a curved design on the handle. Someone stole the knife, Lindy. It was stolen because someone meant to use it to kill your father. And my husband is going to ... to ...'

Lindy rose and drew Sylvana from her chair.

170

They stood there for a moment facing one another: two women, outwardly little difference between them—and worlds apart.

'Will you do something for me?' Lindy asked her.

'I will do anything.'

'Will you go home and leave me to talk to my father about this?'

'What will you do by talking? The knife, as he will find out, is my husband's.'

'Did anybody know that the knife was kept in the drawer of your husband's desk?'

'Anybody would know, if they looked in the drawer. We did not tell anybody, because you do not tell people where you keep all your things. The drawer was never locked. If someone opened it, they would see the knife. And you will find that the knife which was used tonight against your father is the knife from the drawer.'

'But nobody will suppose that your husband—'

'They hate him!' cried Sylvana fiercely. 'They hate Luis because he is little, and fat, and not beautiful. They despise him. And because I knew that, I was ashamed of him, a little. I wished that I had not married him. But now . . . I do not wish that. I do not care what they say about him. I know, inside here—' she thumped her chest with a tiny fist—'here I know that he is a good man. He is not a murderer, no matter what they may say. He is not!'

'Will you tell me something?' Lindy asked.
'What is it?'
'What were you looking for yesterday in my father's desk?'

Sylvana made no answer for a time; then she put a question in her turn.
'Did Athena tell you that?'
'No. Mrs Verney and I saw you. We opened the door of the study and ... and you seemed anxious not to be seen, and so we shut the door again. You went away with Mr Searle.'
'Did you tell your father?'
'No. I told—'
'Since you know so much,' broke in Sylvana, 'do you know this: that this is not the first attempt that has been made on your father's life? Do you know that somebody tried, yesterday, to kill him?'
'Yes.'
'Do you know how? Yes, you will know; if your father told you so much, he would have told you everything. What you do not know, what he does not know is that someone else saw that wire.'
'Mr Searle?'
'Yes. And he had to tell me, because ... because if Mr Barron did not return, somebody—perhaps the police—would find a letter that I had written. It was a letter which your father could have read and understood well. But read after his death by others, or by the police ... that would have been dangerous.

Robert Searle knew what I had written; I had told him. But he found no opportunity, until I was going away from this house yesterday, to tell me that an attempt had been made on your father's life. Then we arranged that we would come back and get the letter.'

'Do you mean that Mr Searle saw the wire and knew that there had been a ... an accident, and made no attempt to help?' Lindy asked incredulously.

'He saw the horse—dead. He saw the wire. He did not think it would be safe to stay until the police came, for he was certain that your father had been killed. So he came back and, when he got an opportunity, he told me that I must get back the letter which I had posted the night before. He said that he would wait outside my house and bring me back here. I came into the house and got the letter.'

'Was it ... was it a threatening letter?' I asked.

She looked at us both.

'I will not tell you anything about the letter,' she said. 'I will say only that it was a stupid letter and I am sorry that I wrote it.'

Lindy asked no more questions. I had nothing to say. Sylvana wrapped her cloak more closely around her, and Lindy led her out into the hall and opened the front door.

'Where is your car?' she asked.

'I left it in the drive of an empty house along the road. I did not want it to be seen.'

'You're not going to walk out there alone,' Lindy said firmly. 'Not with knife-throwers about. We'll walk to the car with you and you can drive us back here.'

When Sylvana had driven away, we shut the door and went upstairs. I felt weary and confused, and my head was beginning to ache. We reached the top of the staircase and from Mr Barron's room we heard Alec Walsh's voice, louder than I had ever heard it. He was speaking with angry emphasis, and Lindy went quickly to the door and opened it. But Alec appeared not to see her; he had caught sight of me in the corridor, and with a compelling gesture, ushered me into the room and threw out his hands.

'You can support me,' he said. 'You can tell this man he's out of his mind. You can make him see that if he doesn't stop this damn-fool procrastination, he'll be dead before anything can be done to find this ... this madman. I've talked to him until I'm tired—now you talk. He's got to see it from the point of view of Lindy and Rex. If he doesn't mind exposing himself to danger, he's got no business to let them stay here and share it. Go on,' he finished in a burst of anger, 'go on; tell him.'

William Barron laughed. He was standing beside Lindy at the foot of the bed; his shoulder was bandaged. He looked very large and very confident and his expression was untroubled. His eyes, watching Alec's angry gestures, had

174

an affectionate glint in them.

'I tell you, Alec—' he began.

Alec Walsh turned on him.

'No. *I* tell *you*,' he corrected. 'I listened to you the last time; now you damn well listen to me. You'll call in the police—or I will.'

'Well, I won't. And if you do,' said Mr Barron, 'you'll be a fool. This isn't a police matter—yet. Some poor deranged devil is having a crack or two at me, and not doing too well. Do you think I'd risk anything, with Lindy and Rex here, if I thought the police could help? If I go to them, what do I tell them? I can't tell them more than I know, which is that somebody's taken a sudden dislike to me. Where does that leave them? Where do they start looking? What do they do—give me a bodyguard? Nobody's going to trail around after me, peering into the middle distance for murderers and getting under my feet—and a bodyguard wouldn't, in any case, have been able to prevent either of these ...' He stopped and looked ruefully at Lindy. 'That was a thin story about my walking through the window, wasn't it?'

'Yes,' said Lindy.

'It was a knife this time—but I didn't want you and Mrs Verney to come in and see it.'

'Where is the knife?' asked Alec.

Rex turned and walked out onto the balcony and came back holding the knife in his hand. I saw that it was not very long, and slender—and

175

had a curved design on the handle.

'The fingerprints on it,' said Mr Barron grimly, 'are mine.' He took it from Rex and stood with Alec Walsh looking closely at it. 'Any idea who'd own a thing like this?'

I opened my mouth and then shut it again, waiting for Lindy to speak. To my amazement, she said nothing—and then I saw that it was because she could not. She was leaning against the rail of the bed, and the deadly pallor of her face appalled me. I was on the point of going towards her, when her look of desperate appeal halted me. She was fighting for control, fighting to keep her momentary weakness from the eyes of the others in the room.

I saw the color coming slowly back to her cheeks and felt that I understood her desire for concealment. If her father had seen her face as I had seen it a few moments before, there would have been no further talk of her remaining in Lisbon. And I knew, now, that in her place I would have wanted to stay and see this thing through to the end—to whatever end.

Alec Walsh was talking.

'Anybody could own it,' he said. 'What we're looking for is not so much who owns it, but who's got that deadly ability to throw it. Knife-throwing—with that accuracy—isn't something you pick up overnight. There's an artist on the job.' He took the knife and looked at the other man. 'I'm going to take this to the police,' he said, 'and nothing you can say will make me change my mind. Do you feel all right now?'

'I'm fine. There was no need to drag you out.'

'I'm glad I came,' said Alec. 'But I'll go now and we can all get some sleep.' He went to the door and looked back at Mr Barron. 'I meant what I said just now,' he said, before he went, one hand still in the pocket into which he had thrust the knife.

Rex went with him. I scarcely heard them go. Lindy looked spent, and I spoke somewhat abruptly to her father.

'Look,' I said, 'she's had enough for one day.'

Mr Barron looked at her with a worried frown. He put out his free arm and drew her to him.

'Wish you hadn't come?' he asked.

Lindy made a strong effort and managed a smile.

'No. Glad,' she said. 'What really happened tonight?'

'I got undressed and opened the door leading to the balcony,' he said. 'I walked out, as I walk out almost every night, to have a smoke before turning in. If I'd lit a cigarette and stood there ... But I put my hand in my dressing-gown pocket and felt for the lighter that's always in there—and it wasn't in there. So I turned to come in—and I turned just in time. I got the knife in my shoulder and the

177

handle hit my face. I swerved and went through the glass of the door. And that's all. Rex came in and we got the knife out and out of sight, before you and Mrs Verney came in.'

'And now,' I said firmly, 'no more.' Rex came in and I went on: 'To bed, both of you— please.' I looked at Lindy's white face and added: 'If you'll get into bed, I'll bring you an aspirin.'

'Bed for everybody,' said Mr Barron. 'But if Mrs Verney wants a nightcap, I can give her one.'

I didn't want a nightcap, but I had an idea he wanted to talk to me. Lindy and Rex went out; Mr Barron watched them go and then shut the door and turned and leaned against it.

'Well?' he asked.

'I agree with Mr Walsh,' I said. 'I'd feel much better if I saw a posse of policemen around the place.'

'Did you talk to Harper?'

'Yes. He seems to think that someone wants to kill you in a hurry. He'll give you his views himself.'

'Who,' he asked in a slow, wondering voice, 'would want to kill me?'

'Could it be ...' I hesitated. 'Couldn't it be somebody in your firm?'

He stared at me as though I had gone suddenly mad.

'In my—In God's name,' he said slowly, 'who in my firm would want to murder me?

Who? Who'd go out and rig up wires? Who'd climb trees at dead of night in my garden and hurl knives at me? And why? I'm a good deal more use to them all alive than dead. I could understand your making a fantastic suggestion like that if you hadn't met them, but—Do they look like thugs? They may have their peculiarities, but—murder! What made you come out with that extraordinary suggestion?'

'I only thought ... they've all got motives, in a way—all except Mr Walsh.'

'Then that makes him the villain, obviously. I presume you leave out Harper? And as Alec Walsh has saved my life in the past, I think we can rule out the possibility that he's trying to deprive me of it now. Who—' his voice was rough with sarcasm—'who's your number one suspect?'

'I didn't have any suspects. I simply—'

'—suggested that there was a murderer in our midst. Well, Searle's capable of anything—but even with Essex coming out over his head, his chances are much better with me in the firm than out of it. Next? Cunha—because I wouldn't have his brother? Or because I'm a philanderer and he's jealous? Cunha's no fool; he knows me well enough to know that I wouldn't look at his wife. I believe in keeping that kind of trouble outside the office. Harper? He wasn't here. That leaves Sylvana and Athena. Well, I wouldn't really like to trust either of them very far, but they can't climb trees and they can't fix wires. And if any of them had wanted to get rid of me, they could have done so before now; I've been at their disposal a long time. And in any case, we don't have to worry about motives when we've got a knife; that's something on which the police will begin to work as soon as Alec shows it to them. The knife—'

'It belongs to Cunha,' I said.

Mr Barron looked at me. I had seen the same look more than once on Henry's face; he fixes it on me when he comes to dinner and praises the soup and asks what it's made of, and I tell him. It's a look halfway between horror and conviction; he would like to assure himself that I'm not serious, but something tells him that I am.

'Cunha?' The word came from Mr Barron at last, on two long-drawn-out syllables.

'Yes. It's his knife. But he didn't throw it.'

'He—'

'No. His wife said so.'

'Look.' He came forward and took me by the arm and spoke in a quiet tone. 'You're worn out. You've been through a hell of a time for the past two—'

'I'm perfectly all right, thank you. I'm merely telling you what Sylvana told us.'

He released my arm.

'Told?'

'Told Lindy and myself.'

'Told you when?'

180

'Tonight.'

'Where?'

'Downstairs in the study.'

'Downstairs in the—But—'

'She threw some gravel up at my window. Lindy and I went downstairs and let her in and we talked.'

'You ... talked. I see. You talked. About knives?'

'There's no reason to look angry. We didn't ask her to come. But she said she had to tell somebody. She was terribly worried because her husband's knife was missing.'

'Missing? You've just informed me that it was sticking into me.'

'She looked for it in the drawer in which it's always kept, and it wasn't there.'

'And where was her husband?'

'He wasn't there, either. She realized that someone had stolen the knife and—'

'—came along to have a chat with you and Lindy? Came along to ask either of you if you'd noticed anybody dead around here? Am I crazy, for God's sake, or are you, or are we all?'

'Please don't shout. I'm perfectly sane. Lindy and I would have told you this when Mr Walsh asked whose knife it was, but I don't think she could bear much more. But we both—Lindy and I—believed what Sylvana said. At least, I believed most of what she said.'

'And will you kindly inform me why, if she was counting knives in the middle of the night and found that one was missing, she came around here to talk to you and to my daughter about it? Why? Why here?'

'Because she and her husband had a quarrel. Athena had been making mischief, and Sylvana thought that her husband might have thought that he had cause for jealousy and—'

'You must be mistaken. Athena knows perfectly well that I—'

'It was Athena who stole my passport.'

'Sylvana told you that, I suppose?'

'No. It was Athena herself who told us, during lunch—but she wouldn't tell us why she'd taken it. So you see, there isn't so little basis, after all, for thinking that somebody in your office was at least connected with these attacks on you.'

'You don't seriously suppose Athena was up that tree tonight?'

'No, I don't. But she might know who was. You can't rule people out just because they don't look like murderers. So on the whole, I'll be very happy when we've got a few policemen on the scene.'

'You'll have your policemen; Alec is seeing to that.' He walked into the middle of the room and stood staring down moodily at the broken glass on the floor. When he spoke again, his voice had lost its harshness. 'Perhaps I won't be sorry to see the police, either, on the whole.' He turned to me. 'What about that nightcap?'

I didn't want one, and thanked him and said

good night. But I didn't go straight to my room; I went to Lindy's and I knocked on the door as softly as possible. If there was no reply, I would go away again. But the door was opened almost at once by Lindy.

'Why aren't you in bed yet?' I asked her. 'I came along to make sure you were asleep. You looked so pale that I felt you needed a nightcap more than I did.'

'I'm ... I'm all right,' she said. 'I just ... felt bad for a few moments, that's all.'

Her voice was shaky, and I saw that she was trembling.

'Get into bed,' I said. 'I'm going to fetch you an aspirin.'

When I got back, she was in bed, but the face on the pillow was still deathly white. I got some water; she took the aspirin and lay back looking at me.

'Now sleep,' I said.

'Yes.' She put out a hand and caught one of mine, and I had a feeling she was holding on to me for support. I sat on the edge of the bed and spoke gently.

'What you're suffering from,' I told her, 'is delayed shock. If you can sleep, sleep; if you can't, come along to my room and stay with me until you feel all right again.'

'I'm ... I'm fine,' she said.

I sat there without speaking for a while. Her eyes were closed, and I hoped that she was dropping off to sleep. But suddenly they opened and fixed themselves on me.

'The knife—' she began, and I interrupted.

'No more knives tonight,' I said.

'No. But it was thrown ... from a tree, wasn't it?'

'Rex thought so. He made a few calculations and thought it must have been the tree that you climbed up to paint the picture of the house.' I glanced at it as I spoke. It was a well-executed piece of work, and I found myself hoping that she would give it to me as a parting present. But she had gone on to speak of Neil Harper.

'You like him, don't you?' she asked.

'Neil? Yes; very much.'

'He likes you.'

'Thank you.'

I saw, with relief, that a little color was coming back into the white cheeks. I sat on, saying nothing, but I knew that she knew that I was there, and I knew she was glad to have me.

I thought that she was asleep, but her eyes opened once more.

'You trust him, don't you?' she asked.

'Neil again? Yes. Implicitly,' I said. 'Anybody would.'

'That's what I thought,' came drowsily from Lindy. 'I trust him, too. He said—do you know what he said?'

'I can guess.'

'He said he loved me.'

'When did he tell you?'

'Tonight, at the theater.'

184

'I see. And you?' I asked.

'From the first moment, when he sat in the train behind his paper, saying nothing at all. From that moment ... forever.'

'Did you tell him?'

'Yes.'

I wanted to ask a thousand questions, but her hand was relaxing in mine, and I saw that she was falling asleep.

I sat on, dreaming. When I was certain that she was sleeping soundly, I crept away.

CHAPTER EIGHT

I was wakened the next morning by the sound of hammer blows on my door. I sat up, my heart thumping in fear, and managed a quavering 'W—who is it?'

'It's me. I. Barron.' His voice, resonant with energy, vibrant with good cheer and heartiness, dispelled my fear, bringing in its place fury at having been so rudely disturbed. 'Are you up?' he asked, between more thumps on the door. 'We're all going on an expedition—hurry up! Can I come in?'

'No, you can't,' I snarled. 'Go away.'

'I'll give you half an hour,' he said.

I made no reply. I heard his amused laughter and his footsteps going down the corridor, and then lay back to compose myself and await my

185

morning tea.

But Lindy was the first person to come in. I saw to my surprise that she was fully dressed.

'What's the matter with everyone?' I asked. I dare say I sounded peevish. I felt peevish.

'Daddy got us up. At least, he got Rex up; I got up at six and went riding.'

'Six! Has everybody gone crazy?'

'No. Daddy's arranged to take us all out. We're taking a picnic lunch.'

'Oh. I hope you enjoy yourselves,' I said, and snuggled down between the sheets.

'You're coming, too.'

'I'm going to stay here and have a nice, quiet day, thank you. Your father may be in an exuberant mood, but I don't feel exuberant.'

'Well, not now, but you will when you've got up.'

'How dare he come and play tattoos on my door before I'm awake?'

'You're lucky he only knocked.'

'What did you go riding at six o'clock in the morning for?'

She smiled. I saw that the fatigue of the previous night had fallen away from her; she looked as fresh as she had on the boat.

'I didn't choose the time. Neil did.'

'He went with you?'

'Yes.'

'When did you arrange it? At the theater?'

'No. We ... we talked to one another on the phone before I went to bed—just before you came in.'

I looked at her.

'But if your father knew that—'

'He does know. I told him. I told him . . . everything.'

'Oh.' I thought it over. 'Is that why he's going around thumping on people's doors?'

'No. That's just because he thinks we all need a change from being gloomy. He thinks that Neil and I . . . He thinks it's too soon. Too soon to know our minds. Too soon—'

'—to have you dragged away from him. I see his point. After all, you've only just arrived and he's only just got to know you.'

'Will you talk to him nicely?'

'I shall talk to him about thumping on my door—but not nicely.'

'And you'll come out with us?'

'I don't like picnics. I'm too old to enjoy them, and I don't like sandwiches. Besides, there's a big party tonight; you've got to be at home making preparations.'

'We're coming back soon after lunch. If you don't go, I shan't.'

'You can't blackmail me. And Rex should have been allowed to sleep late. He was overtired last night.'

'He slept in Daddy's room.'

'He slept where?' I asked in surprise.

'In Daddy's room. He couldn't go off to sleep properly, and Daddy went in and took him into his room . . . Here's your tea. See you

187

later.'

There were no further disturbances, and as I drank my tea and began to feel more human, I regretted having lost the chance of seeing something of the country. It would have been an opportunity of getting away from Lisbon, and I would have enjoyed the drive, especially in the Barrons' luxurious car.

I went downstairs to find the three members of the family halfway through breakfast.

'You're late,' Mr Barron told me. 'You haven't time to eat much; we're setting off at nine-thirty on the dot. And Alec Walsh is coming. And so, for reasons unspecified, is Harper. Harper told me on the phone that you had a hankering to see the old fortification at Torres Vedras, so that's where we're going.'

'Good,' said Rex, with such genuine satisfaction that I choked back the denial I had been about to make.

We set out in two cars; we looked so unlike the people who only a few hours ago had stood upstairs speaking of murder, that I realized how wise Mr Barron had been to get everybody out of the house. For a few hours, we could be at ease. He drove off with Lindy and Rex; Alec Walsh drove his own car and I sat beside him; Neil Harper sat behind.

It was glorious weather. The reports from home were of fog and sleet and bitter cold; here we drove in sunshine and warmth. The countryside seemed to glow; I thought of the snow-covered ground at home and looked out enchanted at the green and fertile country through which we were driving; I saw grapes, olives, apples, lemons, tangerines, acres green with every kind of vegetable. We did not hurry; Alec drove at a moderate pace, sometimes stopping to point out any specially good view; I found his quiet commentary interesting. Neil said nothing; glancing back once or twice, I saw that his eyes were closed; this time, I made no mistake as to what he was thinking about.

We didn't see the other car until we reached Torres Vedras. We drove up a winding road to the top of a hill and there we saw Mr Barron's car; beside it, under the pines, were spread rugs, and on the rugs were the picnic baskets and two interesting-looking wicker-encased demi-johns of wine. Mr Barron and Lindy and Rex were nowhere in sight; Neil and Alec went to look for them. On his return, Mr Barron said he would conduct me around the fortifications.

We walked and we walked and we walked. A student of history would without doubt have welcomed this opportunity to study on the spot the masterly strategy that resulted in the defeat of the French troops and the continued use of the port of Lisbon as a supply base for Wellington's army—but as I looked at the ditches into which William Barron was peering with such interest, I couldn't for the life of me see what had alarmed Massena so much.

'—from here, at Torres Vedras, to Alhandra,' he was saying. 'You attending to me?'

'Yes, of course. But I was thinking—'

'Well?'

'They don't look very formidable now.'

'Formidable? Why, they—'

'I know. Massena took one look and departed.'

'He did nothing of the kind. He sent for reinforcements. They didn't come. He waited for six months—and what happened then?'

'Well, he went off.'

'Where to?'

'Who cares?'

'You should care,' he said. 'You're standing on historic ground. If the French had got through, if Lisbon had fallen, if the British had been driven out of Portugal—Good heavens, don't you know anything?'

'I know quite a lot,' I said, 'I just can't see anything here that would have frightened Massena, that's all.'

'Can't you use your imagination?'

'Of course I can. But—'

'Look here.' He picked up a stick, cleared a piece of ground and proceeded to draw a map of Portugal. 'Now, here is where we are now. There's Lisbon—down there. The British are being supplied through Lisbon, and Wellington has to prevent the French from breaking through. So he builds his defenses from here—are you looking?—right across to Alhandra—there.' He dug a hole with the stick. 'Now do you see how that puts a stop to an advance on Lisbon?'

'Yes, but—'

'It was a magnificent piece of strategy. Don't you know they made Wellington the Marquis of Torres Vedras?'

'I'm glad.'

Mr Barron threw down the stick in disgust and brushed his hands.

'I'm wasting my time,' he said. 'Women amaze me; they seem totally unable to take in the simplest ideas—if the ideas are impersonal. If the Iron Duke had built a harem up here instead of fortifications, you would have been interested in every last little detail. You would have eaten it up. You—'

'Speaking of harems,' I said, 'are you glad about Lindy and Neil?'

'Is that what he means to do with her?'

'Don't be silly. Are you going to be nice to them, or are you going to be—'

'To be?'

'Overbearing.'

'I've just got my daughter out here. She—'

'She loves him.'

'She's nineteen.'

'So was I. And I hadn't one tenth of Lindy's good sense. He's a fine man and—'

'How do you know? Oh, of course.' His voice was heavy with sarcasm. 'You spent

191

three days with him, on board. Same table, too. You get to know everything about a man, just watching him eat. I suppose you encouraged them.'

'I would have done if I'd seen it coming. What possible objection could you raise?'

'You mean I just hand her over—just like that?'

'Not at once. But you accept him as a suitor, you help them, you—'

'All right, all right. I get a daughter, I lose a daughter—and I smile.'

'Yes. You've got Rex.'

He said nothing, and we walked slowly back down the slope. The others were seated on the rugs, taking food out of the baskets; Alec Walsh was uncorking one of the demijohns.

'Where've you been?' he demanded. 'We thought you were lost.'

'So she was,' said Mr Barron. 'None of all this meant a thing to her!'

'Or to me,' said Lindy loyally. 'Neil and Rex fought the whole campaign all over again, and I stood there starving. Come and eat.'

It was a good thing, I reflected, that I hadn't offered to help cut the sandwiches. There were no sandwiches; this picnic wasn't one of those simple ham-and-lettuce affairs. I was given a tiny table which unfolded to disclose an enormous plate; on this Lindy piled cold chicken, cold turkey, ham and tongue, a green salad glistening with oil, and then slices of bread and butter. Alec poured out red and white wine and we were ready to begin. To go on with, there was a cold cheese pie, cream cheese in little cases with sugar to sprinkle on top; there were piles of fruit and hot coffee. I wondered if Wellington had sat up here and enjoyed his food as much as I was enjoying mine. I hoped he had; he deserved it for digging all those ditches.

I never enjoyed a meal so much. When it was over, all I wanted to do was lie back in the sun and doze—but Mr Barron had other ideas. We were not going to lie in the sun; we were going on, almost at once, to a place a little farther north, called Obidos.

'Some other time,' I said.

'You're coming,' he told me. 'You'll like it very much; it's a little walled town and there's a castle there—restored. The Moors built the walls, but they were restored in the twelfth, fourteenth and sixteenth centuries.'

'Well, thank you for telling me,' I said. 'I'll wait for you here while you drive on and look at it.'

'Come on,' commanded Mr Barron. 'Up and on.'

So we went to Obidos. This time, I sat beside Mr Barron in his car, and Rex sat behind. We were hurrying now, for there was not much time, and when I saw Obidos, entirely circled by ramparts along which I knew Mr Barron would have insisted on leading me, I was glad that there would be time for only a superficial look round.

We went over the castle—now a *pousada*—and I enjoyed looking through the rooms, which were well arranged and comfortable. I was dismayed, however, to learn that we were to climb by various difficult and dangerous stone stairways to the roof. My progress was less than dignified, but I was glad I had come, for the view from the top was magnificent—half Portugal seemed to be laid at our feet.

Nobody was in a hurry to go down again. I stood at one of the corners, and Mr Barron came across and stood beside me.

'Enjoying it?' he asked.

'Very much, thank you. It's been a lovely trip. It was a good idea of yours.'

'Had to think of something,' he said. 'The atmosphere in the house was getting a bit too tense for my liking. Noticed the protective attitude Rex has taken up? He's clinging to me like ... like a—'

'Bodyguard. Can you blame him?' I asked.

'I wish to God,' he said moodily, 'that I'd never brought them out here. No—I don't wish that; I only wish they hadn't come out to this mess. I suppose they'll have to be sent somewhere until it's over—one way or the other,' he ended grimly.

'You'll find it difficult to move them.'

'I suppose so.' He stared bleakly across to where Lindy stood with Alec Walsh. 'I'm

194

beginning to lose my grip—a bit,' he said after a time. 'At first I thought there was something rather stimulating in the thought of somebody's wanting to put an end to me. But now . . . I don't find it at all exhilarating. Being a father cramps a man. Without Lindy and Rex, I might have enjoyed it, but now I feel I'd like to live a bit longer and enjoy being a parent. And I was thinking, in the early hours of the morning, that I don't feel I've done anything to deserve this. I've done a lot, I suppose, that I ought to be sorry for, but I can't think of one single act that would make anybody but a madman want to . . . to rub me out. I don't mind a good fight, even at my age, but it has to be a clean fight. This idea of a lunatic lurking somewhere and working in secret . . . no. I haven't deserved it. So perhaps the best thing would be to take the children and do a trip somewhere—anywhere. Show them Portugal. If I stay here, I'm going to have Rex ill on my hands. A boy can't stand this kind of strain for long.' He paused and looked down at me. 'I wish to the devil you weren't going. I suppose I couldn't induce you to stay?'

'No,' I said. 'First, because this is a problem I can't help to solve; second, because you've got to accept the full responsibility of fatherhood. If that sounds heavy, I'm glad; it's a heavy responsibility.'

'You don't approve of me much, do you?'

'I don't know you—much.'

'Oh, I forgot; you haven't spent three days on a liner with me and got to know me thoroughly. But you think that Lindy and Rex could have done better as regards a father?'

'There's nothing the matter with you as a father—once you've realized that you *are* a father.'

'And because I'm a father, do I have to dodge behind a palm pot every time I see an attractive woman coming?'

'Yes. You do.'

'I could marry her, I suppose,'

'You could eventually, but having brought Lindy and Rex out here, it wouldn't hurt you, would it, to spend some time getting to know them?'

'You didn't ever teach in Sunday School?'

'Never. I just happen to like old-fashioned things like quiet, decent living. But if you want to go for the rest of your life behaving like a superannuated Casanova, there's nothing to stop you.'

The sound of his laughter brought Lindy and Neil over to us.

'Something amusing?' she asked.

'Yes. Mrs Verney,' her father told her. 'Why can't we keep her with us?'

'Two reasons, sir,' said Neil. 'One's called Sue and the other's called Theobald.'

'Over my dead body,' I said, and looked at Lindy. 'If there's to be a party this evening, isn't it time to set off for home?'

'In a few moments,' said Mr Barron. 'Just give old Zandro time to finish pointing out the sights to Rex.'

'Zandro?' I repeated.

Mr Barron looked startled.

'Did I say that? I'm glad Alec didn't hear me; he gets annoyed if I use the name; says he's getting too old for nicknames.' He raised his voice and called across, 'You ready, Alexander?'

We all clambered down, and Alec Walsh offered to set off at once with me in order to go the long way around and show me something of the town of Caldas da Rainha.

'Would you like that?' he asked.

'I'd like it very much,' I said. 'But I think I've been invited—'

'Yes,' broke in Mr Barron. 'Mrs Verney's due for tea at the Cunhas; I want her to see his trees; they're worth a visit. I told them I'd send Harper with her. If you'll drop her at their house, Alec, Neil will meet her there.'

Alec and I drove away, but we had no time to do more than drive slowly around Caldas da Rainha; then we were speeding towards Lisbon at a pace that made conversation difficult. I was not sorry; the lunch, the walking and the climbing had made the prospect of a quiet nap very welcome. I was prepared to doze all the way home, but I was roused, presently, by Alec's voice.

'What do you make of it all?' he asked.

197

His tone was sober; there was no need to ask him what he meant. Life, at the moment, was not a matter of picnics or of sight-seeing; this had been an interlude, and a pleasant one; we had been reprieved for a time, but we were going back now to discover what dangers still threatened William Barron.

'I don't make anything of it,' I said. 'All that makes me happy is that Mr Barron seems to have got a bit of sense into his head at last.'

'How?'

'He's proposing to go away somewhere with Lindy and Rex. All that childish, see-if-I-run-away attitude seems to have gone, thank goodness.'

He threw me a swift, unsmiling glance.

'It wasn't an attitude, you know.'

'You mean that's the real William Barron?'

'Yes.'

'You like him very much, don't you?'

To my astonishment, the answer was long in coming—so long, that I thought he had not heard me. Then I heard him repeat the question, almost as though he were asking himself.

'Like him? He's the greatest friend—in a way, the only friend I ever had. I admire him more than I can say. He's...'

He stopped, but I saw that his mind was still on William Barron.

'You saved his life once, didn't you?'

He gave a short, dry laugh.

'Not at any great risk to myself. I'm not one of those fool heroes like Searle. Saving Bill's life ... anybody could, anybody would have done it. But I couldn't save him from trouble. He's not an Irishman, but he's got some of the more belligerent Irish traits. People only have to trail their coats.'

I sat back, listening. I had turned a key and opened a door into the past; Alec's mind had gone back to the days, long before the war, to the beginning of his friendship with William Barron. I was content to sit and listen and learn something about another side of Lindy and Rex's father.

'People call him, sometimes, a ladies' man,' said Alec, 'but nothing was ever further from the truth. Women have always liked him because he was big and powerful and handsome in a rugged sort of way—but no woman ever kept his attention if there was anything in the nature of a fight to be had. He liked people; he liked them and took them on trust and went on liking them until he found them out. We had some good times. When he suggested my joining him here in Lisbon and becoming a member of the firm, I was grateful, because I hadn't many prospects at home.'

'Did you know his wife?'

'Yes. She was a nice woman, but they should never have married. She loved him, but she was too gentle for a man of his type. For a woman like her, it must have felt rather like being tied

199

to a performing animal. He was always up to
something, and her idea of a quiet married life
went to the wind. I think she would have come
out to him in these last years—if he'd asked
her. But he didn't. Sometimes I think that it
simply didn't occur to him. I don't think he
would have thought of having the children out
here if I hadn't told him I thought it would be a
good thing—for him and for them.'

'I'm glad they came. At least, I would have
been glad if they hadn't arrived just as all this
trouble began. Mr Walsh—'

'Well?'

'You know Mr Barron as well as anybody
does, and you know more about his life than
anybody. Haven't you any idea about—I
mean, when he says that he hasn't any enemies,
he must be wrong. Your friends don't try to kill
you. Don't you know anybody who has cause
to hate him?'

'No,' said Alec instantly. 'No, I don't.
People, some people, dislike him; he's high-
handed, and people don't care to be ridden
over, but he doesn't make real enemies,
dangerous enemies; and as far as I know, he
hasn't any. That's to say, I don't know
anybody who hates him enough to want to kill
him. Is that what you wanted to know?'

'Yes. But—'

'But what?'

'If somebody has tried twice in two days,
shouldn't he—for the children's sake—go

away at once? He talked of going, but he said nothing definite. If you could talk to him, persuade him to leave Lisbon ... There isn't any need for him to wait even one more day, until I've sailed. I could go to a hotel.'

'Lindy wouldn't hear of it, and neither would Bill. But if it'll make you feel any better, I'll talk to him. I can put your mind at rest on one point: the police are on the job.'

'The police?' I drew a long breath of relief. 'I'm so glad.'

'So am I. I was a fool to let Bill override me for so long.'

'When did you—'

'I went to them early this morning and gave them the whole story. Does that make you feel better?'

'Much better.'

We were entering Lisbon; soon we were climbing up the winding streets to a point high above the city. The road leveled, and Alec turned into a drive, and I saw before us a large white house. In front of it was parked Neil Harper's car.

'That was quick work,' commented Alec, as Neil came up to us.

Neil grinned.

'Lindy drove Mr Barron's car on the way back. We moved.'

'I see.' Alec laughed. 'There's a lot of her father in that girl. Well, I'll leave Mrs Verney with you, Neil.'

201

He drove away, and Neil led me towards the steeply sloping garden.

'I'll show you a bit before Cunha gets a chance,' he said. 'His trees are his hobby, and he's a bit long-winded when he takes people down to see them.' He stopped at the top of a precipitous path. 'Pretty, isn't it?'

I looked around. We were halfway down the garden; from where we stood, we were already too low to see more than the upper windows of the house, and these were half hidden by the thick foliage of the trees surrounding us.

It was not my idea of a garden. There was not a flower in sight. There were only trees: trees slender or spreading, trees bare or with leaf-laden branches, trees I recognized and trees I had never seen before. Perhaps Henry is right about my lack of intellect, for although I listened to Neil as he reeled off names and characteristics, I couldn't, at the end of it, have answered one question about any one of the trees. I was half afraid that Neil was going to probe, to see how much I had taken in—but he had looked at his watch, and I knew by his sudden increase of speed that we had been wandering down there too long. My feet could have given as clear an indication as his watch.

We walked up the slope and he looked at me with a smile.

'What have you been saying to Lindy's father?' he asked.

'About you and Lindy? I told him it was an

ideal arrangement.'

'You must have said it with some force. His attitude has changed a good deal since this morning.'

'I'm sorry for him—in a way.'

'So am I. To have Lindy snatched away from him, to have her going away...'

He fell into a reverie; when he emerged, I conveyed my good wishes for his happiness, and then we hurried up the last few yards of path and came out onto the terrace that stretched along the front of the house. We paused to glance at the view; although the house stood on the same slope as Mr Barron's, the outlook from each was widely different.

'I prefer the view you get from Mr Barron's house,' I said. 'You can see more of the water.'

We were walking towards the house, and I directed my steps to the drive with the idea of approaching the front door. Neil, however, drew me back.

'Not that way; I know them too well to stand on ceremony,' he said. 'I'll take you in by the door over there, which goes straight into the drawing room.'

'The open one?'

'Yes. If there was time, I'd suggest your going around the house with Sylvana, but I'm afraid we'll have to leave fairly soon. We—'

He stopped. For one instant we stood still on the flagged terrace, everything swept from our minds but the sound that had come at that moment from the room towards which we were walking.

It was a cry—the cry of a man in agony. It came again, and then Neil had sprung forward and entered the room—and I was on his heels.

We found ourselves in a room that looked as though a tornado had swept through it. Chairs were overturned, tables pushed aside; rugs and ornaments and overturned flower vases were moving about the floor, pushed by the flailing legs and arms of two men lying locked in a desperate struggle. They were Luis Cunha and Robert Searle; it did not need more than a glance to see that Searle was uppermost and that Cunha was taking terrible punishment. Standing with her back to the wall, white-faced and shaking, was Sylvana; as we came in, we saw her hand go out and grasp a heavy brass ornament. Before Neil could reach her, she had taken a step forward and brought it down on Robert Searle. For a moment he seemed to be motionless, and then he rolled slowly off Cunha and slumped to the floor and lay there with eyes closed.

There was silence, broken only by Cunha's labored breathing. Sylvana seemed incapable of movement. Neil walked forward, rolled Searle on to his side and bent down to examine the long, bloody gash on his head.

'Ring that bell,' he said to me, with a jerk of his head towards a long bell cord.

I pulled it. A manservant entered and stood

transfixed, until Neil, with a few rapid words of Portuguese, brought him to himself and sent him out, to return in a moment with another servant. Between them they lifted Searle onto the sofa; Sylvana stood with her arms around her husband, trying with her tiny form to support his stout one. Neil went to them, and with the help of the servants, led Cunha out and upstairs to his room.

'Doctor,' he threw at me over his shoulder as he went.

I looked at Sylvana. She was standing still, staring straight in front of her; then her eyes went to Searle's unconscious figure and she gave a long shudder.

'Doctor,' I said.

She looked around with dazed eyes and then picked her way across the littered room to the telephone. As she replaced the receiver, Neil came into the room and spoke to me.

'Take Mrs Cunha into the study and keep her there; give her a drink of some kind,' he ordered. 'I'll see to her husband—and to Searle.'

Without a word, Sylvana turned and led me across the hall. She opened the door and I found myself in a large, overfurnished study. I made her sit down, and sat on a chair near her; then I remembered my orders, and got up and looked around to see whether any drinks were kept in the room. I opened a cupboard, saw some bottles and glasses, poured out a drink and carried it to her.

'I think you'd better drink this,' I said.

'No.' She got to her feet and went towards the door. 'No. I must go to Luis.'

Before she could open the door, it was opened from outside by Neil; he stood there barring her way.

'Not yet,' he said. His voice was gentle. 'You can't do anything until the doctor has fixed him up. Luis is all right; he's been knocked about, but not seriously. You're not—' he gave her a smile—'going to be a widow, so don't look so frightened.'

He shut the door, leaving us together. Sylvana walked slowly back to her chair and sat down. For a long time neither of us spoke. I think she was too dazed to think clearly, and I kept my mouth firmly shut because I knew that if I opened it, a torrent of questions would come forth—and I didn't think she could stand questioning just then. So we sat there, and I looked at her and brooded on the fearsome sights I had looked on during the past two days.

I used to read detective novels. I used to take a couple of them to bed with me and sip a warm drink of milk or lemon juice and lie there comfortably, reading about the pools of blood on the carpet and the bullet wounds, and the cord around the victim's neck. But not any more. Those cozy evenings go on, but I've taken to biographies of the milder kind. I can't read horrors any more. I can't read of the pools of blood without seeing the trickle of blood coming from under Mr Barron's bathroom door. I can't read of knife wounds without seeing Lindy and her white, exhausted look. And when I read about blunt implements, I see Sylvana Cunha poised with a heavy brass ornament in her hand.

Now I sat with the picture of Searle, with Cunha at his mercy. I found myself trembling, and wished that I had poured out two drinks instead of one.

'I hope,' said Sylvana slowly, out of the silence, 'that he is dead.'

With two men lying wounded, it was not possible to decide which one she meant. Her next words cleared up the mystery.

'But I don't think,' she said broodingly, 'that I hit him hard enough.' She raised her eyes and stared at me. 'If I had not done that, he would have killed Luis.'

I said nothing, but I believed her. I did not know what had roused Searle, but I had seen enough to know that he was in a mood to kill.

'Why,' I asked, 'did he attack your husband?'

'Because Luis accused him of trying to murder Mr Barron.'

Into my mind came the picture of the lame man and his meeting with his brother. I could make no sort of connection with the encounter and the accusation—and then I heard Sylvana speaking again.

'You asked me,' she said, 'what I was looking for on Mr Barron's desk. I will tell you now. I was looking for a letter which I had written to him.' Her black eyes were on me, wide and horrified, but I saw that there was no longer any fear in them. 'I had written to him—an angry letter. It was not anger for myself; it was anger because I did not think that Robert Searle had been treated fairly. You see only one side of William Barron; you do not see the other side, the side which is hard and cruel. He brought Robert Searle out here with promises, and he did not keep them. He promised that he would be a partner, and then he changed his mind. It would have been easy, it would have been kind, to tell Searle this, but Barron did not do so. The first knowledge that Searle had of this man who was coming, was on the day on which Alec Walsh and my husband went to London to interview him—and then Mr Barron told Searle, without regret, without sympathy. When Searle told me, I was angry. I was angry with Barron. I was angry with my husband, who had told me nothing of the matter. I thought Searle was a—at that time, I liked him—and I sat down and wrote a letter to Barron. I could have told him what was in the letter, but he would not have listened to me; he would have heard nothing of what I wished to say. So I put in the letter all my hatred of him, because when I was writing, I hated him. It was a stupid letter, but when I had sent it, I felt better. And then when Mr Barron was missing, Searle came to me and said that I must get the letter back. I thought that he was afraid for me, and I was grateful—but now I know that he was afraid for himself. Because in the letter I had written not only of my own hatred, but also of Searle's—and it was for this that Searle wanted nobody to see the letter.'

She stopped. The tears rolled down her cheeks and she brushed them aside with an angry gesture.

'But why did your husband—' I began.

'Today, Searle came here to see me. He came to talk about Barron. He had told me that he was coming; I did not want to see him, but my husband said yes, let him come. When he came into the drawing room . . . I do not know how it began, but suddenly my husband was talking to him and saying . . . terrible things. He told him that he had put the wire across the path. He told him that he had tried to murder Mr Barron. He—'

'But how did your husband know this?'

'He told Searle that, too. Searle was seen by Mr Barron's groom.'

'Mr Barron's—But if the groom saw him, why didn't he tell Mr Barron? Why—'

'He was afraid. Mr Barron can be violent, and the groom was afraid that if he went to him and told him that he had seen one of the members of the firm . . . He was frightened. So the man went to somebody he knew would believe him, to somebody who had known him all his life, to somebody who had got him the job with Mr Barron—he went to my brother-in-law, Fernando Cunha. He told him what he had seen, and Fernando sent for Luis, and they talked to the groom at his home, which is—'

'Yes, I know. I've seen his home,' I said.

'I did not know anything of what my husband was saying to Searle. I listened with horror, and then suddenly Searle had thrown himself on my husband, and ... and—It wasn't a fight, Mrs Verney. It was murder—this time, for my husband. He could do nothing ... nothing. I was sure that Searle would kill him, and I put out my hand and picked up something heavy and ... you saw.'

The account was at an end, but I was where I had been at the beginning—at sea. If the groom had seen Searle, if he had told Cunha what he knew, why had Cunha remained silent? If he knew that Searle had made one attempt on Mr Barron's life, why had he given him the chance to make a second? Why had—

I could make nothing of it. I had tried, not once but many times, to grope my way through the fog and had found myself in deeper obscurity. I was not going to confuse myself further.

A servant came to summon Sylvana; the doctor had come. I went into the hall and saw Neil coming down the stairs; he went into the drawing room and after some hesitation, I followed him. He nodded to the servant who had been watching beside the sofa, and the man withdrew. Neil stood looking down at the inanimate form of Searle.

Presently I saw Searle's eyes open. He lay looking up at Neil for some time.

'The doctor'll be down in a moment,' said Neil. 'He's with Cunha.'

'Is he ... bad?' asked Searle.

'Not too bad.'

'Pity. Pity I didn't kill the swine.'

'You'll have another chance, I imagine. How d'you feel?'

'Take Barron a message from me, will you?' asked Searle.

'If it isn't too blistering.'

'Tell him that he and his firm can go to hell. Tell him I'm getting out. I wanted to tell him before, and I ... I didn't. Tell him he can have his new man and they can both go to hell together.'

'Anything else?'

'Yes. You can go to hell with them. And you'd better tell Barron that Cunha said I tried to murder him. That means that the little swine made the attempt himself and is trying to tie me in on it. And now you can get out.'

Neil went out of the room, taking me with him. He led me to the front door and opened it.

'And now we'll go home,' he said. 'I imagine you've had about enough for one afternoon.'

211

We got into the car. Neil took the wheel and drove without saying a word. After a time, I asked a question.

'How is Cunha?'

'All right. Face bashed a bit. I thought he might have a broken jaw, but it's in one piece. I had a talk with him while we were waiting for the doctor.'

'What about?'

He threw me an enigmatic smile.

'This and that,' he said.

'All right; keep it to yourself,' I said. 'Someday, I hope someone will write to me and tell me who tried to kill Mr Barron. I know, in spite of what Sylvana told me just now, that it couldn't have been Searle. You wouldn't walk out of the house and leave a murderer to—'

'Murderer? Mr Barron is still alive.'

'Well, did Searle try to kill him?'

'No. Not Searle.'

'Do you know that for a fact, or is it just theory?'

Neil stared ahead at the road.

'Theory?' he echoed. 'Yes, that's—No,' he corrected himself. 'No. It's more than that. It's sound enough—except for one thing.'

'What thing?'

'No motive. No possible motive. No shred of motive anywhere. And if you can't find a motive, you can't find the key.'

He sounded so dispirited that I turned to stare at him. I saw that he was pale, and there were lines around his mouth. I remembered that he had a new interest in Mr Barron, and I knew that he was working for Lindy's happiness, struggling to cut a way through the net that surrounded us all.

'It's worrying you,' I said gently.

'It's worrying us all, isn't it?'

'Yes, but need we worry any more? The police are on the job. Alec Walsh has called them in, and we can leave them to clear everything up—can't we?'

He made no reply, and after a time I put another question.

'What did Mr Cunha say to you?'

'Cunha,' replied Neil, 'is a very happy man.'

'Happy? After being manhandled by Searle?'

'He got a bit knocked about, but he got his mind put at rest.'

'How?'

'Because he had imagined lately—and with some reason, I fancy—that his wife had been seeing a little too much of Searle. And Searle's a fine, upstanding fellow and—'

'—and Sylvana hit him with a brass idol and proved that she loved Luis best, after all. Does that get us any nearer to knowing who tried to kill Mr Barron?'

'No. I can't really say that it does.' He sighed. 'Don't say anything to Lindy. I'll tell her about it when I see her this evening.'

I was only too ready to agree to say nothing.

I wanted to get to the *Casa Roma* and lie down and rest. The thought of a party, in circumstances like these, seemed fantastic.

We sat without speaking until Neil drew up at the house.

'We'll be meeting shortly,' he said. 'Give my love to Lindy.'

'I will. I can't say I'm in a party mood.'

'You'll have to pretend. This is a special occasion. The party's being given to launch Miss Belinda Barron into Lisbon society.'

He had handed me out and was seated once more at the wheel.

'If you're planning to marry a girl,' I told him, 'it's as well to get her name right.'

He looked at me in surprise.

'Lindy's short for Belinda, isn't it?'

'Sometimes. But in this case, it's short for Melinda.'

He stared at me, and I saw that he was sitting very still.

'Melinda?' he repeated slowly. 'Melinda?'

'Yes.'

'It's a somewhat ... unusual name, isn't it?'

'It isn't common, I suppose, but I know two other Melindas.'

'Is there ... is there any more of it?'

Somehow, I knew that he was waiting with more than normal interest for my answer.

'Is there any more of it?' he repeated.

'Yes. She's called Bel-Melinda. Perhaps the combination's rather uncommon.'

'Bel-Melinda with a hyphen?'

'Yes.'

'And Bel with one l, or two?'

'One.'

He drew a long breath and settled back in his seat.

'Why did you ask?' I asked him.

He stared at me, but I don't think he really saw me. He answered the question in an absent voice.

'Because,' he said slowly, 'there had to be a motive.'

The car moved forward.

'You mean—' I shouted angrily.

'Yes,' came his reply, wafted by the breeze.

CHAPTER NINE

Perhaps murder was in the air. At that moment, I could cheerfully have murdered Neil Harper. But he was out of reach, borne away in the gray car; I would not see him again until the party was in full swing, and there would be no hope, then, of getting anything out of him.

I stood there quivering with frustrated curiosity, and then I turned and went into the house—and promptly forgot everything as I looked with delight at the scene before me.

The house, always lovely, was in party dress.

Standing in the hall, I gazed at the banked flowers, the softly lit drawing room and dining room and study, all flower-filled. I saw small tables with snowy cloths, silver trays with tall glasses waiting to be filled, the dining table drawn out to its full length, gleaming with silver, gay with color. I went slowly through the rooms and out onto the terrace; here were more tables, more flowers; tubs of ferns in two rows led to a little garden bar.

I walked slowly indoors, my spirits rising with every step. This was the home to which Lindy and Rex had come—gracious, elegant, hospitable. Tonight there would assemble a number of people, old and young, to meet them and perhaps to become their friends. Mr Barron could be, would be an affectionate father. There was nothing to worry about; he and Lindy and Rex would be happy together here, and when Lindy married Neil, as I was certain she would, she would not be going far away.

If the dark shadow passed. At that moment, I was certain that it would. I could not look at the quiet beauty of the rooms without feeling certain that the Barrons would walk in them in unity and happiness. I could not guess who or what threatened William Barron, but at that moment I told myself that nothing would hurt him.

It was in this mood that I dressed. Lindy came in to show me her gown, and she looked so beautiful in it that I went over and kissed her.

'Has your father seen you yet?' I asked her.

'Yes.'

'What did he say?'

She laughed.

'Nothing. He did just what you did.' She paused on her way out. 'Oh, Mr Cunha might not be able to come.'

I made no reply, but Lindy was not waiting for one.

'He isn't very well,' she went on. 'Was he all right when you were at the house?'

'Not very,' I replied.

I waited for her to say that Mr Searle, too, might find himself unable to attend the party, but Lindy did not mention him. Instead, she spoke of Charles Essex.

'His plane's delayed, but nobody seems to know quite how much,' she said. 'Neil's going to the airport to meet him.'

'What time will people begin to arrive tonight?' I asked.

'About nine. Supper's at midnight.'

She went out, and I settled down at the dressing table to put into effect some of the hints Athena had given me on how I should make myself up.

And then Athena walked in.

She came in without knocking. She closed the door behind her and came slowly across the room and sat on the bed. I glanced up as she entered, and then looked away again, unable to believe, unable to bear the picture she presented.

She was in a magnificent, low-cut dress; around her neck was a collar of pearls. Her hair was beautifully done, and crowned with a tiny, twinkling tiara. And in between the collar and the tiara was her gray, ghastly, ravaged face.

I picked up a little jar—I don't know what was in it, but it didn't matter; my hands were shaking too much to allow me to unscrew the top. My eyes were on my own reflection, but next to my face in the mirror was that other, staring sightlessly ahead—the face of a woman already dead.

I felt horror taking possession of me, and fought back to self-control. I began to speak, but Athena was saying something.

'Don't take any notice of me—please. Just go on with ... with whatever you're doing.'

'I ... I won't be long,' I said. My voice sounded high and unnatural, but I was relieved at being able to get the words out at all.

'It doesn't matter,' she answered mechanically.

I knew she had not heard what I said, and cast about in my mind for a subject—anything, anything to break the tension.

'Lindy's ready; she's downstairs. Would you like to go down and—'

'No.'

I turned.

218

'Athena, are you ill?'

She seemed to drag her eyes around to me.

'What?'

'You look ... ill.'

'Leave me alone, will you?' There was anger in her tone, but it was dull and heavy. I stood up with sudden decision.

'Look,' I said, 'I'm going to—'

'Shut up,' she said evenly.

I went back to the dressing table and began to make up my face. I felt weak with pity for her. I didn't know what had happened or what she had seen—or done; I knew only that I had never seen such pain on a woman's face. She sat there, staring straight ahead and saying nothing; there was something animal-like in her dumb suffering.

When I was ready, I walked to the foot of the bed.

'Athena—'

She turned with a swift movement.

'I can't go down,' she said. 'I can't. I tell you I can't.'

'You don't have to go anywhere,' I said. 'You can stay here, but will you let me bring you something? A drink?'

'No. Don't go away for a minute. Don't go.'

I sat on the bed beside her, saying nothing. She put her arms behind her and leaned on them, and then she let her weight fall back, and lay on the pillows, staring at the ceiling. I got up and switched off the big light, leaving the bedside one on, and then felt sorry I had done it, for the shadows fell on her face and made it look more corpselike than ever.

'Go down,' she said presently, 'whenever you want to.'

'I'm in no hurry. This party isn't for me; it's for Lindy and for Rex. I needn't do more than put in an appearance. Mr Cunha,' I added, 'isn't coming.'

'I know. I . . . went there.'

'To the Cunhas'?'

'Yes. I was to . . . to drop in on my way to the party. I was to have drinks with them. Sylvana rang up to ask me. I was to go there and we were all to come on here together. Like . . . almost like friends. I went. But—no drinks.'

'How is he?'

'All right. He's all right. Searle's all right. Sylvana—pretty little murdering Sylvana— she's all right.'

'I was there when she hit Searle. She had to do it.'

Athena's arms were stretched above her head; her fists were clenched.

'I wish I could be dead,' she said slowly. 'I wish I could die now. Now. If I could die now . . . if I could—'

She stopped and, turning her body, lay face down. I saw her shaking and heard the tearing sound of the sobs she was trying to smother. I turned and went out and walked to the head of the stairs; I could hear the buzz and murmur of voices below, the tinkle of glasses and noise of more and yet more guests arriving.

I drew back; I had meant to ask Lindy to send up a drink for Athena to my room, but now I remembered that there was a bell in my room, and all I had to do was to press it and a servant would answer. In the long years of attending to my own needs, I had forgotten this rub-of-the-lamp technique.

I turned to go back, and heard Neil's voice on the stairs behind me. I waited for him and he came up and stood beside me.

'I thought you were going to meet Charles Essex,' I said.

'I put out that rumor,' he said, 'with intent to deceive. Why aren't you downstairs?'

'Athena's with me. I think she's ill.'

His eyes met mine; he said nothing, and I saw that he had gone to one of the far places he visited in order to do his thinking. It was no use trying to reach him; all one could do was await his return.

'Where did you—'

'She's lying on my bed,' I told him. 'She looks like death.'

'Like death?' he nodded slowly. 'Yes, that's about it. Like death. Will you go back to her? I'll bring her up a drink.'

I went back. Athena was lying in the same position, but now she was very quiet. The tiny tiara had fallen off and lay on the floor. I picked it up and put it on the dressing table and stood looking at it.

There was a soft knock at the door, and Neil came in with a tray on which were three glasses. He gave one of them to Athena.

'Drink this,' he said.

There was a moment's hesitation, and then she sat up and faced him, heedless of her ravaged appearance. Her hair was hanging down, her eyes red and swollen. She sat looking at him listlessly, and there was something so uncharacteristic, so hopeless in her lack of concern for her looks, that I felt my heart growing heavy with pity. She was almost unrecognizable, but Neil gave no sign.

'Drink up,' he said.

She drank swiftly, and gave him back the glass.

'You shouldn't have come,' he said.

'What else did you think I'd do?' she asked him.

He seemed to have no answer to this. I got the feeling that they were saying things I could not hear. Something had come into the room with Neil, some air of inevitability, as though there were nothing surprising in Athena's appearance, or in her misery and her hopelessness. Fear stirred in me, but I did not know what I was frightened of.

'You're not going to the airport,' said Athena. It was a statement and not a question. 'Who's going?'

'Searle's going.'

'Clever, aren't you?' said Athena. She covered her eyes with her hands and spoke with them hidden. 'And we just wait, and do nothing? Oh God!' she whispered softly.

Without uncovering her eyes, she twisted around and lay once more on the pillows. Neil handed me my drink, signed to me to drink it, and finished his own. Then he took me outside and shut the door behind us.

'I'd like to stay with her,' I said.

'I assure you that you can do nothing for her. The only thing—' He paused and looked down. 'You're crying,' he said.

'I am not.' I dabbed my eyes angrily. 'You'd cry, too, if you had any feelings. She's in trouble, and I don't like walking out and leaving her.'

'I think it would be kinder to leave her.'

'But she's—'

I stopped. There had been a sound behind me, and I did not need to be told what it was; it was the sound of the key being turned in the lock of my door.

I walked down the corridor beside Neil.

'There are a great many things,' he said as we reached the head of the staircase, 'that it's impossible to explain at this—'

'I don't want to know anything,' I said. 'I don't want to know what it was that made her look like that. I don't. I don't.'

'Then we can go downstairs.'

We walked on. It was only one flight of

223

stairs, but it was like a journey from one world to another; from the quiet of my room to the beat of a dance band; from despair to dancing. The beauty of the scene was enhanced by the brilliant colors of women's dresses and the glitter of jewels, but I could think of nothing, now, but Athena, locked by herself in my bedroom.

We became part of the gay, laughing crowd. I looked around and saw young men and girls of every type; I heard English and American, Portuguese, Spanish, French and German. Lindy was flushed with happiness. Rex stood beside his father in a corner of the room and both were watching her smilingly. I saw Sylvana pass; she was in a dress so diaphanous that it seemed to float; I felt that it needed a room all to itself. Across the room I saw Alec Walsh's tall figure. Beside him was a girl in her late twenties; tall, slender, beautifully dressed. I wondered who she was. He saw me, and with a word to her, made his way across to me.

'Dance?' he asked.

'No—oh no! Thank you!' The words came in a rush, and in so decisive a tone that I hurried on in an effort to soften their effect. 'I gave up dancing a long time ago.'

'If you won't dance, will you have supper with me?'

'I'd love to.'

'Then I'll look for you later.'

He bowed and returned to the girl across the

room, and the long, affectionate, intimate look they exchanged made me long to turn and walk out of the room, away, up to my room, far from the noise of gaiety. Alec Walsh—and that tall, graceful girl ... and upstairs, Athena, with her ravaged face. I knew, now, who the girl was; I did not need to be told. Alec's eyes as he looked at her, his air of quiet proprietorship, his hand under her elbow steering her towards the softly lit garden—everything spoke of an understanding, an intimacy.

I felt sick and shaken. There was nothing out of the way about it, I told myself; I had seen disappointed love in many forms. Athena was not the first woman who had lost the man she wanted to someone younger and fairer. I was aware that with all her grooming, Athena, beside this fresh, glowing girl, would appear as nothing more than well preserved. And Alec—he was not the first man who had ventured to marry a girl many years his junior; and despite his age, he looked young in face and figure, and I knew how much fascination he would exercise over a girl—over any woman. Athena had lost, as other women had lost, and there was no need for me to have this sense of foreboding; she would get over it. Alec had not been her first love and he would not be her last.

But as I said the words to myself, I knew that I did not believe them. I believed that she loved him—deeply and lastingly. Her mistake had not been in loving too much, but in hoping too much. She had seen her own good looks, and thought them a match for his own. They had known one another, liked one another, for years; they had interests in common stretching beyond the firm. She had thought it certain that they would marry; she had not thought of a girl in a pale green gown, with the clear good looks and the smooth skin of youth.

She was upstairs, lying on my bed—and Alec was in the garden with the girl in green.

I heard Neil speaking beside me.

'I wouldn't worry too much,' he advised.

'Perhaps, after all, it's a man's world,' I said. 'Are they engaged?'

'Unofficially. You won't be having supper with him. Mr Barron is having all the members of the firm in the study, to welcome the new fellow. You're invited.'

'Thank you. Why don't you go and dance with Lindy?'

'Because I promised her I'd look after you. What are you hiding behind the curtain for? Come out and let people see you. You look too nice to be hidden away.'

'I don't feel nice. I want to be upstairs with Athena. I want to tell her—'

'Well? What would you tell her?'

'Nothing.'

'Quite right.' His tone was gentle. 'There's really nothing to say. Come into the garden. It's cool, but it isn't really cold.'

226

We went outside, and in the doorway I brushed against a man who was coming in.

'You mustn't run *him* down,' said Neil, steering me past him.

'Why not? Exiled royalty?'

'No. He's a policeman.'

'A ... a what?' I stammered.

'Policeman. And so's the fellow over there— and there. You didn't expect them to come in uniform, did you?'

'I—You mean the police are here?'

'Certainly. Mr Barron's here, isn't he?'

'Yes, but ... but do you mean that they're here tonight in case anybody ... in case somebody—'

'Exactly.'

'But ... but nobody could possibly—Why, there must be over two hundred people here! You don't imagine, do you, that somebody's going to ... to attempt to throw knives at Mr Barron in ... in public!'

'There are curtains in the rooms; people can hide behind them. You were doing it yourself. There are bushes in this garden; Mr Barron has several times this evening been standing with his back to one of them—and a man has been in the bushes behind him, within striking distance. But the man in each case, fortunately, has been a policeman, ready to strike anyone who might attempt to strike Mr Barron. But you see that—as you might say—danger lurks?'

227

His tone was as expressionless and as unreadable as ever. I turned to face him.

'Do you expect anybody to ... to make an attempt tonight?'

'I do.'

'Is that a supposition, or a conviction? I mean, do you seriously—'

'Quite seriously,' he said.

I took my time before speaking again. I wanted to be sure of speaking in a normal voice; I didn't want to croak with terror or scream with horror, and I knew that for the first few moments I was capable of doing either or both.

'Do you understand,' I said slowly at last, 'that I am a guest at a party at which my host might at any moment be ... be—'

'Your host has been in grave danger ever since your arrival.'

'But—a trap laid for him out there on a lonely hillside, or a knife thrown in the night ... perhaps. But not now. Not in ... in—No.' I drew a long breath. 'No, it's too fantastic. You're only saying it to keep my mind off Athena, and I'm grateful to you, but there's no need to overdo it.'

'My habit of restraint,' said Neil, 'is well known.'

'Are you trying to ... to warn me?' I asked.

'Yes.'

'Am I,' I quavered, to my everlasting shame, 'am I in danger too?'

228

'I think not.'

'And Lindy and Rex?'

'I hope not.'

'Then why are you trying to frighten me?'

'Because you are one of the people here tonight who know that two attempts have been made on Barron's life. A third will be made tonight—and soon. I have told you because there are many pairs of eyes watching him— and watching the people around him. Another pair will be useful.'

I stood there and let panic engulf me. There have been times in my life when I have found it best to go under, to be submerged without struggling; to struggle is to invite exhaustion. The wave would wash over me, and it would recede.

It receded, and I found myself thinking clearly. I was trapped in a case of murder. I—and Lindy and Rex. I couldn't get out, even if I wanted to. I, Katrina, widow of the late, bitterly lamented George Verney, was at a party in a foreign land with a number of guests, one of whom might at any moment make an attempt to murder the host. The man standing beside me had, quietly and unemotionally, told me so. The man standing beside me...

My thoughts paused. The attacks on Mr Barron had begun two days ago. Two days ago, the man standing beside me had landed in Lisbon. Two days ago...

'Don't look at me like that,' came Neil's

229

voice. 'But you really should have thought of it before. You're much too trusting. But when you come to think of it, when that little trap with the wire was arranged, you and I were on the *Juan Cortez*. And I couldn't really have thrown the knife, because I was out with you and Lindy, and there wasn't time for me to have got up that tree. But, as I say, you ought to have looked at my credentials before.'

I had nothing to say. I turned to go in, but a man was coming up to us—a lame man. It was my third look at Fernando Cunha; I had seen him first across a piece of waste ground, and then I had seen him crossing the street as I stood with Athena. But I had not had so near a view before.

He stopped before me and gave a little bow.

'You are Mrs Verney,' he said.

'Yes.'

He smiled, and his face, even less handsome than his brother's, lit up in the same unexpectedly charming way. Sylvana floated up and put a hand on his arm, and they walked away together.

'I didn't expect him to be here,' I said.

'He wasn't invited,' said Neil.

'Then—'

'Sylvana asked if she might bring him—to escort her. She didn't think her husband would be able to come. But this is one party, I fancy, that he won't miss. Here's Mr Barron.'

'What are you two hatching out here?' asked

230

Mr Barron. 'It's nearly time for supper. And it's time your friend Essex turned up.'

'Which reminds me, sir,' said Neil, 'I learned something today. But—' he smiled as Rex came up—'it isn't fit for the ears of a young man.'

'Want me to withdraw?' smiled Rex.

'No.' Neil turned to Mr Barron. 'What I learned,' he told him, 'was Lindy's full name.'

'Lindy—Melinda, Bel-Melinda,' said her father. 'A rose—and so on.'

'Bel-Melinda's a very unusual name, isn't it?' asked Neil.

Mr Barron stared at him, and some of the color left his face. His voice, when it came, had lost its heartiness and was cool and distant.

'Very uncommon, I should say.'

'I suppose,' said Neil, 'you wouldn't care to tell me where you came across it, sir?'

'No, I wouldn't.' Mr Barron flushed and seemed to recover himself. A smile touched his lips. 'At least, I wouldn't,' he amended, 'in front of this young fellow here.'

'Don't mind me; go ahead,' invited Rex.

'All right; I will,' said his father. 'It was before I met your mother; keep that well in mind. I hadn't set eyes on your mother. I was young and free and heart-whole. And I took a great fancy to—guess who?'

'Bel-Melinda,' said Rex.

'Right. And nothing whatsoever came of it—in an amorous way. Just happy companionship. And then I met your mother and all that remained of Bel-Melinda was her name. But I thought, and your mother thought that the name was a pretty one, and so we named our first child Bel-Melinda. During the war years, I saw a good deal of the other Bel-Melinda—but that was just happy companionship, too, even though she did look wonderful in uniform. After the war, she vanished—I never found out where.' He turned to Neil. 'And that's how Lindy got her name,' he ended.

'It interested me,' said Neil slowly, 'because I had only once before heard it.'

Mr Barron's eyes were suddenly eager.

'When my father mentioned it. He heard it,' said Neil, 'in the course of a murder trial.'

It seemed a long time before Mr Barron spoke. His eyes had never left Neil's face.

'Go on, will you?' he asked quietly.

'A woman was being tried for murder,' said Neil. 'My father was the judge. Her name was Bel-Melinda. Her Christian name. Her full name was Bel-Melinda Essex, but the Bel-Melinda was a little too much for the reporters; they referred to her throughout the trial as Mrs Essex.'

'*Essex!*' echoed Mr Barron in a stunned voice. '*Essex?*'

'She was the stepmother,' said Neil, 'of the young man who's arriving shortly to join the firm: Charles Essex.'

I can still see the scene. I can see Rex, interested but puzzled. I can see Neil Harper looking like a human oyster, and Mr Barron staring at him incredulously. He was trying to read behind the words, trying to project his mind into the past and recall Bel-Melinda, trying to link what he remembered with what he had just heard. And we were waiting for Neil Harper to go on—but Neil appeared to have said all he intended to say.

I saw a question on Mr Barron's lips, but he had no time to utter it; a servant had come into the hall and was striking a gong—long, echoing sounds to indicate that it was midnight and supper was being served. Mr Barron put his hand for a moment on Neil's arm.

'We'll have a talk about this,' he said. 'And now let's go along to the study; Essex ought to be here any moment.'

Rex at his heels, he made his way through the guests who were crowding into the dining room, and went to the study. Neil put a hand on my elbow and I was about to let him steer me in the same direction, when someone halted me.

'Look!' I said.

He looked. Athena was coming down the stairs, her head held high. The despairing, agonized woman on the bed had vanished; this was Athena as I had seen her first; self-confident, assured, even arrogant.

I saw Sylvana cross the hall and walk up to

the foot of the stairs. Athena came down and stood beside her and they looked at one another—a long, level glance which I could not read, but in which I was surprised to see very little animosity. They walked together towards the study, and then I saw Sylvana swerve in order to go across the hall and meet a man who had just entered the house. It was her husband, Luis Cunha; his head and his neck were bandaged, but between the bandages, his face had a calm and smiling look. With his wife, he followed Athena into the study, and Neil and I went in after them.

When we were all in the room, Mr Barron came in and shut the door behind him. I saw that with the exception of Searle and the newcomer, Charles Essex, all the members of the firm were present. Lindy was standing beside her father; Rex was seated on the corner of the table, one leg swinging.

'Well, we're all here except Searle and Essex,' said Mr Barron, looking around, 'but with Essex, we're in the same plight as the small boy who put on his mother's glasses: no object in view. Alec, did you put a call through to the airport?'

'Yes. The plane was in; they ought to be here soon,' said Alec.

'I don't see why we shouldn't have a drink while we're waiting,' said Mr Barron. 'Cunha, what's this I hear about your having had a fall?'

'In the drawing room,' said Cunha. 'It was

nothing.' He hesitated. 'My brother is here; perhaps you wouldn't mind if—'

'Bring him in,' said Barron.

Senhor Cunha went out and returned in a few moments with his brother Fernando; they stood on either side of Sylvana, their stoutness and solidity emphasizing her slender loveliness.

Neil poured out a drink and took it to Athena.

'This how you like it?' he asked.

She took it, but made no attempt to drink. She held it and listened to Neil talking, but I knew that her mind was not on what he was saying; she was looking everywhere but at Alec—but there was no need, I saw, for her to avoid his glance; he had not looked at her since she entered the room. He brought me a drink and then joined Lindy at the table on which the tray of drinks was placed.

'Can't I have the same as Sylvana?' she asked.

Alec smiled and shook his head.

'No. Too strong.'

'Aunt Kate—' she turned and called to me—'I'd love something really strong; what do you advise?'

'A squeeze of lemon and a nice long drink of water,' I said.

Mr Barron laughed, and our eyes met across the room, and I was startled to see in his a look of something that was not admiration, but a sentiment I valued more; gratitude and—almost—affection. It lasted only a moment, but I was glad that I had seen it. Then he had turned to listen to Alec's quiet voice.

'If we can't drink to Essex,' said Alec, 'we can drink to Mrs Verney and to her speedy return to Portugal.'

He handed Mr Barron a drink and raised his own.

'Mrs Verney,' he said. 'A good journey over to her grandson and a speedy return to Lisbon.'

'Mrs Verney,' said Mr Barron, and raised his glass.

There was a choking cry, a shout—and two screams. And then dead silence.

And in the horror-laden pause that followed, I knew that murder no longer lurked among us. It had closed in—at last.

CHAPTER TEN

I don't know how long we were standing there, but to the end of my life I shall have no difficulty in regrouping the tableau we presented. At the time, I had no notion that I was seeing anything; I stood frozen with fear and horror, waiting for something to happen—something terrible. There was no clear thought in my mind, no impression of anything but the suspense that hung over us all. But as I look back, I see every detail of the picture. I see Mr Barron with the drink in his hand. I see Lindy, chalk-white by his side. I see Rex staring at them. I see Neil Harper, who had leapt with incredible swiftness across the room and was standing on the other side of Mr Barron. The cry had come from Lindy, the shout from Luis Cunha. The screams had come from Sylvana and—I learned afterwards—myself.

Mr Barron was the first to move. He stared down in stupefaction at his daughter and seemed almost too dazed for speech. Lindy put out a hand and seized her father's wrist.

'Don't ... don't drink it,' she said in a choked voice. 'Don't.'

'Don't drink it?' echoed her father. 'Don't—In God's name, what's come over you?'

'Don't drink it.' Lindy could only repeat the words. 'Don't, I tell you.'

'Are you mad?' her father asked in a dazed voice. 'What are you trying to say,'

'She's quite sane,' came Neil's voice. 'Please—' He reached across and took the drink from Mr Barron's hand and held it carefully.

Behind me, there came a sudden movement; somebody had opened the door of the study violently. I turned to see that Athena had gone out and was running with short, awkward steps towards the staircase. Luis Cunha took a step forward.

'Let her go,' said Neil quietly. 'Rex, will you follow Mrs Rodrigues and see that she's all right? She's been taken … ill.'

Rex would have given much to disobey, but there was something in Neil's voice that sent him out of the room without argument. He paused at the door and looked around as though unwilling to go alone, and after a glance at Neil, Fernando Cunha walked to his side and went out of the room with him.

'Lock the door, Lindy,' said Neil.

Lindy locked it, and I heard Mr Barron's voice, cold with rage.

'Will somebody explain this … this—'

'Yes; I will,' said Neil. 'The drink you had in your hand a moment ago is poisoned.'

Mr Barron pivoted slowly around to face the speaker. His eyes were blank with bewilderment, but I knew that he had no thought of doing anything but believing the quiet words Neil had uttered. His rage had passed; his body was tense with expectation.

'Do you know … who?' he asked.

'Yes. We all know—except Mrs Verney,' said Neil. 'And you would have known before, if I had thought that you would believe anything but the evidence of your own eyes— and your own ears. The drink was mixed in this room—for you. The poison was dropped into the glass—for you.'

'Who?' shouted Mr Barron suddenly.

238

'Who—who, who?' His eyes went wildly around the room. 'For God's sake, who? Who did it?'

'I did it,' said Alec Walsh.

Hazily, because everything was hazy at that moment, I saw William Barron turn slowly to face his friend. Alec Walsh met his gaze levelly and then he smiled a slow, grim, bitter smile.

'I did it,' he repeated quietly. 'I put the wire on the path. I threw the knife. I poisoned the drink.'

'You're ... you're insane.' The words came from Mr Barron in a hoarse whisper. 'You're drunk, Alec—or you're ill. That's it; you're ill. You're—'

'No,' said Alec.

'You—No,' said Mr Barron. 'No. There's something—You're covering up for someone else. You're—Oh, for God's sake, Alec, stop this!'

'You've got to hear it,' said Alec, in the same level tone. 'I didn't want to kill you, but I had to.'

'He's crazy.' Mr Barron had swung around to appeal to Neil. 'Tell him he doesn't know what he's saying, Neil—tell him! We're friends, he and I, friends—do you hear me? We're friends! We're old friends, old comrades. He and I ... we're—To stand there and talk of killing me, it doesn't even—He's ... he's—'

'He had to kill you,' said Neil. 'You—or Charles Essex. I think he must have thought, first, of killing Charles Essex in London, but there was no time, no opportunity, no occasion. And that left him with the only alternative—to kill you.'

'Why?' The question was not addressed to Neil. It was a cry from William Barron to Alec Walsh. 'Why?'

Alec closed his eyes for a moment and then opened them and fixed them on the other man.

'You were the only one in the world,' he said, 'who could have told Essex who murdered his father.'

'But I don't know who murdered his father? *He* doesn't know who murdered his father! The police don't know! The police—ask Neil there—are looking for a foreigner, a—'

'The police,' said Alec, 'are looking for a man named Zandro.'

There was silence. Mr Barron's face was gray. Luis Cunha went forward and put a chair behind him and pushed him gently into it. Alex began to speak quietly.

'Only two people in the world knew who Zandro was,' he said. 'You—and Bel-Melinda, who first gave me the name. My letters to her, which Charles Essex found after her death, could not have led the police to me. There was no clue—only the name. They might have got part of the way, but no more. But when I knew that Essex was coming out here, I knew that sooner or later, you would call me Zandro ... and Essex would hear you. He would learn that your daughter's name was his stepmother's: Bel-Melinda. He would learn that you had known her before her marriage. You would tell him that the three of us—you and I and Bel-Melinda—had been friends, good friends, good companions, throughout the war. It wouldn't have taken him long to find out what you didn't know: that I had followed Bel-Melinda to England, that I'd looked for her—and found her. I found her too late. She was married and she had a stepson, who was away at school.'

'And you ... you killed her husband,' whispered Mr Barron. 'You killed Bel-Melinda's husband.'

'Yes. Not in envy. Not even in an attempt to clear the way to marrying her. She didn't love me and she didn't want me. I killed him in a moment—just one moment—of blind disappointment and rage. Disappointment because I had made no impression on her, and rage because he tried, in a clumsy way, to find out whether there was anything between Bel-Melinda and myself in the past. He couldn't, or wouldn't believe that there had been nothing—and he went too far. I ... I attacked him. I didn't know I'd killed him. I left England the next day to join you here in Lisbon, and then I read that he had been killed and that Bel-Melinda was to be tried for murder. And ... I stayed here. I'd seen enough to know that things were pretty good for you out here. They were good for you, and they could be good for me. I reminded myself that I had saved your life—saved you to enjoy the sweets of life. Why should my life come to an end because a jealous man had attacked me? I wanted to live as you were living; had to choose between that—and going back. The choice didn't take long. I stayed, and it would have been all right if a damned twist of fate hadn't brought young Essex out here. When I knew that he was coming, my first thought was to get rid of him—somehow, anyhow, by any means. My next idea was to do away with myself. But ... I'd found a new reason for living. I wanted to live and to love and to have children—and I knew that I could have all these if only I could prevent you and Essex from meeting. But I knew something else, too: I knew that you would have forgiven me for the murder of a man, even if the man were Bel-Melinda's husband—but you would never forgive me for letting her stand trial for the murder I'd committed.' His mouth twisted in a ghastly attempt at a smile. 'And so ... I had to kill you.'

The room was very quiet until he spoke again, this time to Neil.

'Before I go ... away,' he said, 'I'd like to know how you ... found out.'

'I didn't find out,' said Neil. 'It was Lindy who found out. After the knife was thrown, Rex telephoned and asked you to come—and you came. Lindy noticed a peculiar mark on

242

the back of your coat; it was the same mark—a three-color paint stain—that she had got on the back of her dress when she had been sitting up in the tree that morning, painting a picture of the house. It was a small stain, but it was quite unmistakable—and so she knew that you had been up in the tree.'

Mr Barron's eyes were on Lindy.

'Why didn't you tell me?' he asked heavily.

'You wouldn't have believed me,' she said. 'So I told Neil.'

Mr Barron looked at Alec.

'What are you going to do?' he asked.

'What does it matter?'

Alec's voice was dull. He was staring down at the desk, and I saw Mr Barron take a step towards him and then stop, his face white and hopeless. My heart seemed to swell as I saw the pain in his eyes—for it was clear that Alec Walsh was not thinking of him. His mind was fixed only upon what he had lost. Bitter, defeated, he was counting his losses—and those which counted least were the ties which had bound him to William Barron. Not friendship, but self-interest. Not affection, but ambition.

I came out of my stupor to see that Alec was at the door. Neil had unlocked it and was holding it open. Alec paused as he passed him, and the eyes of the two men locked for an instant. I could read nothing in Neil's, but I heard Alec's brief, bitter laugh.

243

'Well ... thanks,' he said.

He took a step or two into the hall, and then stopped. Robert Searle was coming toward him, and with Searle was a tall young man who, at the sight of Alec, quickened his step and went up to him with outstretched hand. But Alec had swerved and was going with long, unhesitating strides towards the front door. He had opened it and gone out; it closed behind him with a dull, terrible finality.

Charles Essex stood looking after him in bewilderment; then Neil took him by the arm and led him into the study. I was at the door and I didn't wait to see him go in, but I often wonder, when I look back, what his sensations must have been as he stood on the threshold and looked into the room. Lindy, her face streaming with tears, stood with her father's arm around her shoulders. Neil was examining with absorbed and somber interest the glass he held in his hand. Strangest sight of all, though Charles Essex could not know that, was Sylvana Cunha in her husband's arms, her hands clinging to him and her head resting upon his chest.

I went out and closed the door, but I didn't go upstairs. I walked into the crowded dining room and found a place at the table and sat unregarded, unregarding, unheeding, unhearing. I let myself float on the sea of sound; I let it fill my ears and my mind and shut out all other sounds and sensations. I sat there

244

until the long supper was over and the guests had gone out of the room; I sat on while the servants began to clear away the food.

Then I went upstairs.

Athena was not in my bedroom; she was standing out on the balcony, staring straight in front of her into the darkness. I walked out and stood beside her.

'Can I do anything?' I asked.

'No. Has he ... gone?'

'Yes. How long,' I asked, 'have you known?'

'I guessed—a little. But I loved him, and I couldn't believe it, and there seemed no reason, no motive ... And then tonight, when I got to the Cunhas, Fernando Cunha told me. He said that Neil wanted me to stay away, to go home—but I wouldn't. I couldn't. I came here with some idea of ... of warning ... of stopping him. But then I knew that nothing could stop him. Once Essex came ...'

We stood without speaking for a long time. Then she put her hands up to her face. When she took them away again, I expected to see tears; but she stood dry-eyed under the light.

'Pray for him,' she said.

'Yes.'

'I wish,' she said, out of another silence, 'that you were going back to England. I would have liked to have gone with you.'

'Are you going to England?'

'Yes.' Her tone was weary. 'I've got to go somewhere, and England is a place where

245

people ... leave you alone. That's all I want now, and forever—just to be left alone. Not to remember him. If I remember, I shall remember that at the end, he didn't love me. He loved that girl. He was going to marry her. He loved her so much that he was prepared to kill Barron ...' She gave a shiver. 'And now.... Do you know that prayer? *May the souls of the faithful departed rest in peace....*'

Faithful departed? He had murdered Bel-Melinda's husband. He had left her to suffer the agony of the trial. He had tried to murder his friend William Barron. He had fallen in love and forgotten Athena's existence. Faithful departed?

'Amen,' I said.

CHAPTER ELEVEN

I never knew exactly how much Rex learned of the events preceding the arrival of Charles Essex. His father may have told him everything; he may have told him a part. But the past came to matter less to them than the future. Lindy's engagement was announced, and nobody wanted to remember what had gone before. Nobody wanted to speak or to think about what had happened.

There was no sense of relief at the clearing up of the mystery; we did not debate or discuss; we

246

had no desire to recapitulate. It was over—but we remembered only that we had liked Alec Walsh. William Barron said little, but he would never, perhaps, be quite the same man again.

Alec's body was washed up the next day on the beach called Guincho. There was an impressive attendance at his funeral; Charles Essex was the only member of the firm who did not follow the coffin.

I spent my last morning in Lisbon at Athena's house. I could do nothing for her except small, practical things; I could help her to pack and I could listen to her when she tried to make plans for the future.

Neil took Lindy and myself out to lunch, and he answered my questions.

'When did you know—for certain?' I asked him.

'At Obidos, when Mr Barron called Alec Zandro. Out riding that morning, Lindy had told me about the stains she had seen on Alec's coat; she had rung me up the night before and we went out riding to be able to talk quietly. I heard about the stains; there was the proof—but where was the motive? Where was the link between the old murder and the new attempt at murder? It wasn't until you told me Lindy's full name that I got what I was looking for. And it explained other things, too, the reason for urgency, for hurry. I was certain that there was a connection between Walsh's visit to London, and the appointment of Charles, and the attempts on Mr Barron's life. I telephoned my father in London; he had told me that the police were looking for a man named Zandro; whom they took to be a foreigner. It all began to tie up: Why should Alec Walsh be so anxious to prevent Charles from coming to Lisbon? Why should he have concealed from Mr Barron the fact that Bel-Melinda was Charles' stepmother? Why—'

'But wait a minute,' I said. 'The groom saw—'

'The groom told Fernando Cunha that he had seen Searle on the path the night before the wire was fixed; he had not known what he was doing there—until he heard the horse scream and went to see what had happened. He saw the wire, and took his story to Fernando Cunha. Fernando sent for his brother Luis. When they questioned the man, they learned that he had only seen the back of Searle—but he was certain that it was Searle he had seen. Luis, with great good sense, told you and Lindy to say nothing; he had no proof, and he knew Mr Barron wouldn't take the word of a groom. So he decided to watch Searle, and then he discovered that his knife was missing.'

'Who—'

'There had been a brief meeting at Cunha's house to discuss Essex and the work he was to do. The meeting took place in Cunha's study; Searle was there, and Cunha concluded he'd taken the knife; he didn't take into account the fact that Mr Barron and Alec Walsh were in the room, too. He was certain it was Searle, and he went out that night and kept watch on Searle's house—and Searle didn't leave the place. The next day, he made the mistake of accusing Searle—with what result, you saw. I don't think Searle would have felt so murderous if he himself hadn't suspected Cunha—and I admit that I wondered about Cunha myself, for a moment; he had waited years for Mr Barron to agree to taking Fernando into the firm, and Mr Barron had just refused. He might have refused in a manner that could turn Luis, or his brother Fernando, into an enemy.'

'But if the groom actually saw—'

'He saw the back of a man he thought was Searle. When I went upstairs with Cunha after Searle's attack on him, I reminded him that from the back, Searle and Alec Walsh looked extraordinarily alike; it was easy to mistake them.'

'I know. I did it myself once—the first time I saw Alec Walsh,' I said.

'What else do you want to know?'

'Why did Athena plant suspicions about his wife in Cunha's mind?'

'Athena,' said Neil, 'was like a wounded animal. She had been hurt, and that made her dangerous. She knew that nobody in the firm had wanted Alec Walsh to marry her, and she struck out meaning to get revenge where she could. She succeeded well enough to make Sylvana believe that it was her husband who might be involved in the attacks against Mr Barron. If any good can be said to have come out of this terrible business, it is that the members of the firm have become better friends than they ever were before. Mr Barron has changed his mind about Fernando Cunha; he's taking him into the firm.'

I looked at them both.

'When you knew for certain that it was Alec, why didn't you tell me?'

Neil smiled gently.

'Because you would have given yourself away.'

'But when you came up to my room and spoke to Athena—you knew then, and you said nothing to me. You let me go downstairs and—'

'If I had told you, could you have gone downstairs and met Alec Walsh and behaved in your usual manner?'

'I—'

'No, Aunt Kate, darling, you couldn't,' said Lindy. 'Your face—'

'—speaks volumes,' finished Neil. 'Didn't your brother ever tell you? Alec Walsh would have looked at you—and he would have known that we knew.'

I was silent for so long that Lindy looked at me in alarm.

'I was only thinking,' I said, 'that in spite of

250

everything, I'm . . . I'm sorry he's dead.'

'I don't think you need be,' said Neil, and his young voice was grave.

'He was—'

'—a murderer,' said Lindy.

'We know that now—but before it all happened, we all thought him good and kind and . . . reliable.'

'That's not quite accurate,' said Neil. 'Cunha never really trusted him. Searle hated him. There was a general feeling—unspoken, but strong—that he wasn't a fellow anybody ever got to know very well. Mr Barron, who thought he knew him, knew nothing whatsoever about him. My guess is that Bel-Melinda was in love with Mr Barron, both before his marriage and after it, but he never thought of her in that way. I think that was why she went away without saying where she was going; she didn't want to see Lindy's father again because he didn't love her; she didn't want to see Alec Walsh again because he did. Alec Walsh followed her—without a word to his friend. He kept his secret for nearly twelve years. He accepted Mr Barron's offer of a partnership, accepted his help and his hospitality—and in the end, tried to murder him.' He mused for a time. 'You know Searle's staying?'

I nodded. I had been present when Robert Searle had come in to say good-by to Mr Barron. I would have gone away, but Mr

251

Barron had waved me back to my chair. Before Searle could speak, he had addressed him.

'Wanted a word with you,' he said.

I saw Searle looking at him with something like shock in his eyes. Mr Barron was not the man he had been before Alec Walsh's death; he had lost none of his brusque manner, but there was far less force behind it.

'I came to say good-by, sir.'

'You needn't have troubled,' said Mr Barron. 'You're not going.'

'I'm—'

'You're not leaving the firm. Not yet, anyhow.'

'I think it would be better, sir.'

'Well, you're wrong. The fact that we got another man in was due, largely, to the fact that you and Walsh never got on. I've talked to Cunha and he agrees with me. Walsh is dead, and the best thing you can do is to stay on and give it another try. Look around and find yourself a wife—plenty of nice girls here in Lisbon—and settle down.'

'I attacked Mr Cunha.'

'And his wife attacked you. Forget it. Go away and for God's sake remember that life's ahead of you and not behind you. Forget you were a war hero; nobody's interested. Keep your mind on the present, and on the job. Help Essex to get the hang of things. Do you want to go on or are you going to stay?'

'I'll—' Searle stopped and cleared his throat.

'I'd like a shot at it,' he said.

When he had gone, we sat in silence. Then Mr Barron roused himself and looked across the room at me.

'I can't talk you out of leaving, then?'

'Thank you—but no.'

'You can't spend the rest of your life visiting your son and daughter.'

'No. I wouldn't be able to afford to shuttle between them, for one thing. When I leave Sue, I'll go back to England and do some work; when I've saved the fare, I'll go out to my son.'

'Haven't you any regular income?'

'No.'

'What happens when you're too old to scrape up these fares?'

'I don't think I'll ever be too old. I think that when I'm too feeble to get up a gangway without assistance, I'll understand that my traveling days are over—and also my years of usefulness—and I shall die a nice natural death in my sleep and not be a bother to anyone.'

'Sleeping pills?'

'Good heavens, no! I said a nice natural death. Face to the wall. *Now lettest Thou Thy servant*, and so on.'

'Your own children are settled and don't need you; you could find a family that did.'

'My grandchildren will need me. Who'll baby-sit? Who'll hear their prayers? Who'll do smocking on their clothes? Who'll read them "Little Boy Blue" and "Little Black Sambo," or whoever the current heroes are? Who'll teach them their ABC?'

'Their parents. Why don't you stay here?'

'Here?'

'Don't pretend you don't understand.'

'I understand that you're still shirking being a father.'

'I won't be a father long. Lindy'll go off with young Harper. And Rex—how much will I see of him after the next couple of years?'

'More than you realize. Children aren't so easy to shake off.'

'You're alone—all alone.'

'And will be forever and ever, Amen,' I said. He looked at me.

'You like it as much as all that?'

'Yes. Living alone is a habit, I think. First you don't like it and then you get used to it and then you find you like it and, finally, you understand that your life is your own. That's a good feeling. Your children draw you, but they have no claim on you any more. You like to visit them, but the thought of giving up—'

'Giving up what?'

'Oh, I don't know. Waking up in a quiet room by yourself. Going home at night to your own fireside, your own company, to books, to a cat and a dog. Solitude, to me, isn't loneliness; it's ... it's what I want.'

'It isn't what I want.'

'You haven't had much family life yet. After a few months of Lindy and Rex, after living with them, living through their problems, living it up, in short, then I think you'll be in a better frame of mind to welcome solitude.'

'Thank you for nothing. What would you do if I asked you to save me from a lonely old age?'

'You've got too much sense. And if you wanted me to relieve your loneliness, you'd have to know me a great deal better and a good deal longer.'

'You think that's important?'

'Very important.'

Mr Barron's lips twisted in sudden pain.

'I knew Alec,' he reminded me quietly, 'for over twenty years.'

CHAPTER TWELVE

When the *Juan Cortez* had docked at Lisbon less than a week before, I had stood on deck looking down at a crowd of people among whom I knew not one. When I stood on the dock waiting to go aboard the *Princess Isabel*, I was surrounded by friends all anxious to keep me with them, all unwilling to say good-by. I wished with all my heart that Henry could see me. Lindy and Rex, Neil Harper, the Cunhas, Luis and Sylvana and Fernando; Robert Searle and Charles Essex. They came with gifts and made their farewells with regret.

Athena was not there. She had sent me a

note and a small package which, on opening, I found to contain a magnificent brooch. It had been, she said, Alec's only gift to her; she wanted me to have it. It was now in the bottom of one of my new suitcases; I had no idea what I would do with it. I would not wear it and I would not sell it. Perhaps Sue, when she was older...

Mr Barron was not there either; he had said good-by, a private one, that afternoon. It had been a brief and quite unemotional farewell, and there had been to my relief, no mention of lonely old ages, his or mine. Neither, somewhat to my chagrin, had there been any word of future meetings; there was not even a reference to my calling at Lisbon on my way home to England. He merely said, without any change in the manner that I knew so well, that I was to be on board promptly and that I wasn't to let Lindy upset me. This referred to a last-minute attempt on the part of Lindy and Rex to make me postpone my departure.

'Good-by,' he said. 'And thank you for having been so kind.'

'I was kind?'

'Very kind.' He held out a hand. 'Take care of yourself.'

And that was all. Even for William Barron, it was somewhat lacking in warmth. When it was over, I started wondering how I felt about it, and couldn't decide. I hadn't wanted much more, but it wouldn't have hurt him, I thought, to say that he was sorry I was going, or that he had enjoyed ... well, nobody could have enjoyed the past few days, but he could have said something warm, something kind. He could have brought me a book to read on the journey—not an expensive book; just a thought. He could have—

Oh well, I told myself, he had more sense than I had; he didn't allow casual contacts to disturb his routine. He was quite right to keep it casual, the low, mean, cold-blooded brute.

Before I went on board, Rex kissed me, to my great pleasure. Lindy gave me a damp embrace. Neil, to my surprise, bent and pecked my cheek. The others shook hands—and then I was going up the gangway and across the entrance hall and to my cabin, to find it vivid with brilliant flowers. One of the cards, I saw with pleasure, was Mr Barron's.

I went up and stayed on deck, waving until they were all out of sight. Lisbon, with its pink-washed look, with its trees and flowers, was left behind. I went down to my cabin and tried to make myself believe that I would always leave a port with friendly handshakes still warm on my palm, with friends waving, with presents in my arms and flowers all around me. That old business of coming and going unregarded—all finished, I said to myself.

And then I mopped my eyes and went on unpacking.

When I went up on deck again, I found that we were no longer in the estuary. We were on the dark, open sea, and the ship was beginning to roll. Lisbon was a wink of lights far away.

The first summons sounded for dinner. I went to the lounge and drank a glass of sherry and tried to feel gay. I was on my way to Sue. Soon I would see my grandson.

I looked around at my fellow passengers and thought that I had never seen such a collection of morons anywhere. All the way across the Atlantic with this bunch ... every day, and at every meal ...

I paid for my drink and walked out on deck. This was the time Lindy and Rex and Neil and I—

None of those over-the-shoulder glances, I told myself firmly. I wasn't going to spend the rest of my life looking backward.

I stood staring over the side. Time passed; the second gong sounded.

I went down at last. A steward was seated outside the saloon, allotting places to the new passengers. I waited my turn and approached him.

'Name, Madam?'

'Mrs Verney. I want a nice quiet—'

He was not running his pencil down the vacant places. He had risen.

'This way please, Madam. We have your seat.'

I followed him, bewildered but

unquestioning. Mr Barron, I reflected, was not likely to allow a friend of his to travel incognito.

We reached the table. It was a table for two. The steward placed me in my seat, and from the opposite one rose a large form, surmounted by a forceful, grinning countenance.

'Ah,' said William Barron. 'You're late.' He sat down and unfolded his napkin. 'I can recommend the olives.' He handed them to me, took one himself, and leaned back in his chair. 'Speaking of getting to know people well . . .' he began.

We hope you have enjoyed this Large Print book. Other Chivers Press or Thorndike Press Large Print books are available at your library or directly from the publishers. For more information about current and forthcoming titles, please call or write, without obligation, to:

Chivers Press Limited
Windsor Bridge Road
Bath BA2 3AX
England
Tel. (0225) 335336

OR
Thorndike Press
P.O. Box 159
Thorndike, ME 04986
USA
Tel. (800) 223-6121
(207) 948-2962
(in Maine and Canada, call collect)

All our Large Print titles are designed for easy reading, and all our books are made to last.